The SCHOLASTIC CLASSICS were chosen very carefully – these are our favourite books, and we want them to become your favourites too. There's a reason they've been around for so long. They're just great stories, no matter how old you are or how long it's been since they were written. They may mean something different to everyone who reads them, but they always mean something.

The books you read when you're young live on in your mind for ever. We think these ones are worth the space.

Oscar Fingal O'Flahertie Wills Wilde was a celebrated playwright, author and poet. He was born in Dublin in 1854, and lived in Oxford, Paris and London. He died in 1900.

THE HAPPY PRINCE

AND OTHER STORIES

Oscar Wilde

Scholastic Children's Books
An imprint of Scholastic Ltd
Euston House, 24 Eversholt Street, London, NW1 1DB, UK
Registered office: Westfield Road, Southam, Warwickshire, CV47 0RA
SCHOLASTIC and associated logos are trademarks and/or
registered trademarks of Scholastic Inc.

This edition published by Scholastic Ltd, 2018

ISBN 978 1407 18450 0

A CIP catalogue record for this book
is available from the British Library.

Printed by CPI Group (UK) Ltd, Croydon, CR0 4YY
Papers used by Scholastic Children's Books are made
from wood grown in sustainable forests.

1 3 5 7 9 10 8 6 4 2

T   its
and   used
f   d,

CONTENTS

The Happy Prince

High above the city, on a tall column, stood the statue of the Happy Prince. He was gilded all over with thin leaves of fine gold, for eyes he had two bright sapphires, and a large red ruby glowed on his sword-hilt.

He was very much admired indeed. "He is as beautiful as a weathercock," remarked one of the Town Councillors who wished to gain a reputation for having artistic tastes; "only not quite so useful," he added, fearing lest people should think him unpractical, which he really was not.

"Why can't you be like the Happy Prince?" asked a sensible mother of her little boy who was crying for the moon. "The Happy Prince never dreams of crying for anything."

"I am glad there is someone in the world who is quite happy," muttered a disappointed man as he gazed at the wonderful statue.

"He looks just like an angel," said the Charity Children as they came out of the cathedral in their bright scarlet cloaks and their clean white pinafores.

"How do you know?" said the Mathematical Master, "you have never seen one."

1

"Ah! but we have, in our dreams," answered the children; and the Mathematical Master frowned and looked very severe, for he did not approve of children dreaming.

One night there flew over the city a little Swallow. His friends had gone away to Egypt six weeks before, but he had stayed behind, for he was in love with the most beautiful Reed. He had met her early in the spring as he was flying down the river after a big yellow moth, and had been so attracted by her slender waist that he had stopped to talk to her.

"Shall I love you?" said the Swallow, who liked to come to the point at once, and the Reed made him a low bow. So he flew round and round her, touching the water with his wings, and making silver ripples. This was his courtship, and it lasted all through the summer.

"It is a ridiculous attachment," twittered the other Swallows; "she has no money, and far too many relations;" and indeed the river was quite full of Reeds. Then, when the autumn came they all flew away.

After they had gone he felt lonely, and began to tire of his lady-love. "She has no conversation," he said, "and I am afraid that she is a coquette, for she is always flirting with the wind." And certainly, whenever the wind blew, the Reed made the most graceful curtseys. "I admit that she is domestic," he continued, "but I love travelling, and my wife, consequently, should love travelling also."

"Will you come away with me?" he said finally to her; but the Reed shook her head, she was so attached to her home.

"You have been trifling with me," he cried. "I am off to the Pyramids. Goodbye!" and he flew away.

All day long he flew, and at night-time he arrived at the city. "Where shall I put up?" he said; "I hope the town has made preparations."

Then he saw the statue on the tall column.

"I will put up there," he cried; "it is a fine position, with plenty of fresh air." So he alighted just between the feet of the Happy Prince.

"I have a golden bedroom," he said softly to himself as he looked round, and he prepared to go to sleep; but just as he was putting his head under his wing a large drop of water fell on him. "What a curious thing!" he cried; "there is not a single cloud in the sky, the stars are quite clear and bright, and yet it is raining. The climate in the north of Europe is really dreadful. The Reed used to like the rain, but that was merely her selfishness."

Then another drop fell.

"What is the use of a statue if it cannot keep the rain off?" he said; "I must look for a good chimney-pot," and he determined to fly away.

But before he had opened his wings, a third drop fell, and he looked up, and saw – Ah! what did he see?

The eyes of the Happy Prince were filled with tears, and tears were running down his golden cheeks. His face was so beautiful in the moonlight that the little Swallow was filled with pity.

"Who are you?" he said.

"I am the Happy Prince."

"Why are you weeping then?" asked the Swallow; "you have quite drenched me."

"When I was alive and had a human heart," answered the statue, "I did not know what tears were, for I lived in the Palace of Sans-Souci, where sorrow is not allowed to enter. In the daytime I played with my companions in the garden, and in the evening I led the dance in the Great Hall. Round the garden ran a very lofty wall, but I never cared to ask what lay beyond it, everything about me was so beautiful. My courtiers called me the Happy Prince, and happy indeed I was, if pleasure be happiness. So I lived, and so I died. And now that I am dead they have set me up here so high that I can see all the ugliness and all the misery of my city, and though my heart is made of lead yet I cannot chose but weep."

"What! is he not solid gold?" said the Swallow to himself. He was too polite to make any personal remarks out loud.

"Far away," continued the statue in a low musical voice, "far away in a little street there is a poor house. One of the windows is open, and through it I can see a woman seated at a table. Her face is thin and worn, and she has coarse, red hands, all pricked by the needle, for she is a seamstress. She is embroidering passion-flowers on a satin gown for the loveliest of the Queen's maids-of-honour to wear at the next Court-ball. In a bed in the corner of the room her little boy is lying ill. He has a fever, and is asking for oranges. His mother has nothing to give him but river water, so he is crying. Swallow, Swallow, little Swallow, will you not bring her

4

the ruby out of my sword-hilt? My feet are fastened to this pedestal and I cannot move."

"I am waited for in Egypt," said the Swallow. "My friends are flying up and down the Nile, and talking to the large lotus-flowers. Soon they will go to sleep in the tomb of the great King. The King is there himself in his painted coffin. He is wrapped in yellow linen, and embalmed with spices. Round his neck is a chain of pale green jade, and his hands are like withered leaves."

"Swallow, Swallow, little Swallow," said the Prince, "will you not stay with me for one night, and be my messenger? The boy is so thirsty, and the mother so sad."

"I don't think I like boys," answered the Swallow. "Last summer, when I was staying on the river, there were two rude boys, the miller's sons, who were always throwing stones at me. They never hit me, of course; we swallows fly far too well for that, and besides, I come of a family famous for its agility; but still, it was a mark of disrespect."

But the Happy Prince looked so sad that the little Swallow was sorry. "It is very cold here," he said; "but I will stay with you for one night, and be your messenger."

"Thank you, little Swallow," said the Prince.

So the Swallow picked out the great ruby from the Prince's sword, and flew away with it in his beak over the roofs of the town.

He passed by the cathedral tower, where the white marble angels were sculptured. He passed by the palace and heard the sound of dancing. A beautiful girl came out on the balcony with her lover. "How wonderful the stars are," he said to her, "and how wonderful is the power of love!"

"I hope my dress will be ready in time for the State-ball," she answered; "I have ordered passion-flowers to be embroidered on it; but the seamstresses are so lazy."

He passed over the river, and saw the lanterns hanging to the masts of the ships. He passed over the Ghetto, and saw the old Jews bargaining with each other, and weighing out money in copper scales. At last he came to the poor house and looked in. The boy was tossing feverishly on his bed, and the mother had fallen asleep, she was so tired. In he hopped, and laid the great ruby on the table beside the woman's thimble. Then he flew gently round the bed, fanning the boy's forehead with his wings. "How cool I feel," said the boy, "I must be getting better;" and he sank into a delicious slumber.

Then the Swallow flew back to the Happy Prince, and told him what he had done. "It is curious," he remarked, "but I feel quite warm now, although it is so cold."

"That is because you have done a good action," said the Prince. And the little Swallow began to think, and then he fell asleep. Thinking always made him sleepy.

When day broke he flew down to the river and had a bath.

"What a remarkable phenomenon," said the Professor of Ornithology as he was passing over the bridge. "A swallow in winter!" And he wrote a long letter about it to the local newspaper. Everyone quoted it, it was full of so many words that they could not understand.

6

"Tonight I go to Egypt," said the Swallow, and he was in high spirits at the prospect. He visited all the public monuments, and sat a long time on top of the church steeple. Wherever he went the Sparrows chirruped, and said to each other, "What a distinguished stranger!" so he enjoyed himself very much.

When the moon rose he flew back to the Happy Prince. "Have you any commissions for Egypt?" he cried; "I am just starting."

"Swallow, Swallow, little Swallow," said the Prince, "will you not stay with me one night longer?"

"I am waited for in Egypt," answered the Swallow. "Tomorrow my friends will fly up to the Second Cataract. The river-horse couches there among the bulrushes, and on a great granite throne sits the God Memnon. All night long he watches the stars, and when the morning star shines he utters one cry of joy, and then he is silent. At noon the yellow lions come down to the water's edge to drink. They have eyes like green beryls, and their roar is louder than the roar of the cataract."

"Swallow, Swallow, little Swallow," said the Prince, "far away across the city I see a young man in a garret. He is leaning over a desk covered with papers, and in a tumbler by his side there is a bunch of withered violets. His hair is brown and crisp, and his lips are red as a pomegranate, and he has large and dreamy eyes. He is trying to finish a play for the Director of the Theatre, but he is too cold to write any more. There is no fire in the grate, and hunger has made him faint."

"I will wait with you one night longer," said the

Swallow, who really had a good heart. "Shall I take him another ruby?"

"Alas! I have no ruby now," said the Prince; "my eyes are all that I have left. They are made of rare sapphires, which were brought out of India a thousand years ago. Pluck out one of them and take it to him. He will sell it to the jeweller, and buy food and firewood, and finish his play."

"Dear Prince," said the Swallow, "I cannot do that;" and he began to weep.

"Swallow, Swallow, little Swallow," said the Prince, "do as I command you."

So the Swallow plucked out the Prince's eye, and flew away to the student's garret. It was easy enough to get in, as there was a hole in the roof. Through this he darted, and came into the room. The young man had his head buried in his hands, so he did not hear the flutter of the bird's wings, and when he looked up he found the beautiful sapphire lying on the withered violets.

"I am beginning to be appreciated," he cried; "this is from some great admirer. Now I can finish my play," and he looked quite happy.

The next day the Swallow flew down to the harbour. He sat on the mast of a large vessel and watched the sailors hauling big chests out of the hold with ropes. "Heave a-hoy!" they shouted as each chest came up. "I am going to Egypt"! cried the Swallow, but nobody minded, and when the moon rose he flew back to the Happy Prince.

"I am come to bid you goodbye," he cried.

"Swallow, Swallow, little Swallow," said the Prince, "will you not stay with me one night longer?"

"It is winter," answered the Swallow, "and the chill snow will soon be here. In Egypt the sun is warm on the green palm-trees, and the crocodiles lie in the mud and look lazily about them. My companions are building a nest in the Temple of Baalbec, and the pink and white doves are watching them, and cooing to each other. Dear Prince, I must leave you, but I will never forget you, and next spring I will bring you back two beautiful jewels in place of those you have given away. The ruby shall be redder than a red rose, and the sapphire shall be as blue as the great sea."

"In the square below," said the Happy Prince, "there stands a little match-girl. She has let her matches fall in the gutter, and they are all spoiled. Her father will beat her if she does not bring home some money, and she is crying. She has no shoes or stockings, and her little head is bare. Pluck out my other eye, and give it to her, and her father will not beat her."

"I will stay with you one night longer," said the Swallow, "but I cannot pluck out your eye. You would be quite blind then."

"Swallow, Swallow, little Swallow," said the Prince, "do as I command you."

So he plucked out the Prince's other eye, and darted down with it. He swooped past the match-girl, and slipped the jewel into the palm of her hand. "What a lovely bit of glass," cried the little girl; and she ran home, laughing.

Then the Swallow came back to the Prince. "You are blind now," he said, "so I will stay with you always."

"No, little Swallow," said the poor Prince, "you must go away to Egypt."

"I will stay with you always," said the Swallow, and he slept at the Prince's feet.

All the next day he sat on the Prince's shoulder, and told him stories of what he had seen in strange lands. He told him of the red ibises, who stand in long rows on the banks of the Nile, and catch goldfish in their beaks; of the Sphinx, who is as old as the world itself, and lives in the desert, and knows everything; of the merchants, who walk slowly by the side of their camels, and carry amber beads in their hands; of the King of the Mountains of the Moon, who is as black as ebony, and worships a large crystal; of the great green snake that sleeps in a palm-tree, and has twenty priests to feed it with honey-cakes; and of the pygmies who sail over a big lake on large flat leaves, and are always at war with the butterflies.

"Dear little Swallow," said the Prince, "you tell me of marvellous things, but more marvellous than anything is the suffering of men and of women. There is no Mystery so great as Misery. Fly over my city, little Swallow, and tell me what you see there."

So the Swallow flew over the great city, and saw the rich making merry in their beautiful houses, while the beggars were sitting at the gates. He flew into dark lanes, and saw the white faces of starving children looking out listlessly at the black streets. Under the archway of a bridge two little boys were lying in one another's arms to try and keep themselves warm. "How hungry we are!" they said. "You must not lie here," shouted the Watchman, and they wandered out into the rain.

Then he flew back and told the Prince what he had seen.

"I am covered with fine gold," said the Prince, "you must take it off, leaf by leaf, and give it to my poor; the living always think that gold can make them happy."

Leaf after leaf of the fine gold the Swallow picked off, till the Happy Prince looked quite dull and grey. Leaf after leaf of the fine gold he brought to the poor, and the children's faces grew rosier, and they laughed and played games in the street. "We have bread now!" they cried.

Then the snow came, and after the snow came the frost. The streets looked as if they were made of silver, they were so bright and glistening; long icicles like crystal daggers hung down from the eaves of the houses, everybody went about in furs, and the little boys wore scarlet caps and skated on the ice.

The poor little Swallow grew colder and colder, but he would not leave the Prince, he loved him too well. He picked up crumbs outside the baker's door when the baker was not looking and tried to keep himself warm by flapping his wings.

But at last he knew that he was going to die. He had just strength to fly up to the Prince's shoulder once more. "Goodbye, dear Prince!" he murmured, "will you let me kiss your hand?"

"I am glad that you are going to Egypt at last, little

Swallow," said the Prince, "you have stayed too long here; but you must kiss me on the lips, for I love you."

"It is not to Egypt that I am going," said the Swallow. "I am going to the House of Death. Death is the brother of Sleep, is he not?"

And he kissed the Happy Prince on the lips, and fell down dead at his feet.

At that moment a curious crack sounded inside the statue, as if something had broken. The fact is that the leaden heart had snapped right in two. It certainly was a dreadfully hard frost.

Early the next morning the Mayor was walking in the square below in company with the Town Councillors. As they passed the column he looked up at the statue: "Dear me! how shabby the Happy Prince looks!" he said.

"How shabby indeed!" cried the Town Councillors, who always agreed with the Mayor; and they went up to look at it.

"The ruby has fallen out of his sword, his eyes are gone, and he is golden no longer," said the Mayor in fact, "he is little better than a beggar!"

"Little better than a beggar," said the Town Councillors.

"And here is actually a dead bird at his feet!" continued the Mayor. "We must really issue a proclamation that birds are not to be allowed to die here." And the Town Clerk made a note of the suggestion.

So they pulled down the statue of the Happy Prince. "As he is no longer beautiful he is no longer useful," said the Art Professor at the University.

Then they melted the statue in a furnace, and the Mayor held a meeting of the Corporation to decide what was to be done with the metal. "We must have another statue, of course," he said, "and it shall be a statue of myself."

"Of myself," said each of the Town Councillors, and they quarrelled. When I last heard of them they were quarrelling still.

"What a strange thing!" said the overseer of the workmen at the foundry. "This broken lead heart will not melt in the furnace. We must throw it away." So they threw it on a dust-heap where the dead Swallow was also lying.

"Bring me the two most precious things in the city," said God to one of His Angels; and the Angel brought Him the leaden heart and the dead bird.

"You have rightly chosen," said God, "for in my garden of Paradise this little bird shall sing for evermore, and in my city of gold the Happy Prince shall praise me."

The Nightingale and the Rose

"She said that she would dance with me if I brought her red roses," cried the young Student; "but in all my garden there is no red rose."

From her nest in the holm-oak tree the Nightingale heard him, and she looked out through the leaves, and wondered.

"No red rose in all my garden!" he cried, and his beautiful eyes filled with tears. "Ah, on what little things does happiness depend! I have read all that the wise men have written, and all the secrets of philosophy are mine, yet for want of a red rose is my life made wretched."

"Here at last is a true lover," said the Nightingale. "Night after night have I sung of him, though I knew him not: night after night have I told his story to the stars, and now I see him. His hair is dark as the hyacinth-blossom, and his lips are red as the rose of his desire; but passion has made his face like pale ivory, and sorrow has set her seal upon his brow."

"The Prince gives a ball tomorrow night," murmured the young Student, "and my love will be of the company.

If I bring her a red rose she will dance with me till dawn. If I bring her a red rose, I shall hold her in my arms, and she will lean her head upon my shoulder, and her hand will be clasped in mine. But there is no red rose in my garden, so I shall sit lonely, and she will pass me by. She will have no heed of me, and my heart will break."

"Here indeed is the true lover," said the Nightingale. "What I sing of, he suffers – what is joy to me, to him is pain. Surely Love is a wonderful thing. It is more precious than emeralds, and dearer than fine opals. Pearls and pomegranates cannot buy it, nor is it set forth in the marketplace. It may not be purchased of the merchants, nor can it be weighed out in the balance for gold."

"The musicians will sit in their gallery," said the young Student, "and play upon their stringed instruments, and my love will dance to the sound of the harp and the violin. She will dance so lightly that her feet will not touch the floor, and the courtiers in their gay dresses will throng round her. But with me she will not dance, for I have no red rose to give her;" and he flung himself down on the grass, and buried his face in his hands, and wept.

"Why is he weeping?" asked a little Green Lizard, as he ran past him with his tail in the air.

"Why, indeed?" said a Butterfly, who was fluttering about after a sunbeam.

"Why, indeed?" whispered a Daisy to his neighbour, in a soft, low voice.

"He is weeping for a red rose," said the Nightingale.

"For a red rose?" they cried; "how very ridiculous!" and the little Lizard, who was something of a cynic, laughed outright.

But the Nightingale understood the secret of the Student's sorrow, and she sat silent in the oak-tree, and thought about the mystery of Love.

Suddenly she spread her brown wings for flight, and soared into the air. She passed through the grove like a shadow, and like a shadow she sailed across the garden.

In the centre of the grass-plot was standing a beautiful Rose-tree, and when she saw it she flew over to it, and lit upon a spray.

"Give me a red rose," she cried, "and I will sing you my sweetest song."

But the Tree shook its head.

"My roses are white," it answered; "as white as the foam of the sea, and whiter than the snow upon the mountain. But go to my brother who grows round the old sun-dial, and perhaps he will give you what you want."

So the Nightingale flew over to the Rose-tree that was growing round the old sun-dial.

"Give me a red rose," she cried, "and I will sing you my sweetest song."

But the Tree shook its head.

"My roses are yellow," it answered; "as yellow as the hair of the mermaiden who sits upon an amber throne, and yellower than the daffodil that blooms in the meadow before the mower comes with his scythe. But go to my brother who grows beneath the Student's window, and perhaps he will give you what you want."

So the Nightingale flew over to the Rose-tree that was growing beneath the Student's window.

"Give me a red rose," she cried, "and I will sing you my sweetest song."

But the Tree shook its head.

"My roses are red," it answered, "as red as the feet of the dove, and redder than the great fans of coral that wave and wave in the ocean-cavern. But the winter has chilled my veins, and the frost has nipped my buds, and the storm has broken my branches, and I shall have no roses at all this year."

"One red rose is all I want," cried the Nightingale, "only one red rose! Is there no way by which I can get it?"

"There is a way," answered the Tree; "but it is so terrible that I dare not tell it to you."

"Tell it to me," said the Nightingale, "I am not afraid."

"If you want a red rose," said the Tree, "you must build it out of music by moonlight, and stain it with your own heart's-blood. You must sing to me with your breast against a thorn. All night long you must sing to me, and the thorn must pierce your heart, and your life-blood must flow into my veins, and become mine."

"Death is a great price to pay for a red rose," cried the Nightingale, "and Life is very dear to all. It is pleasant to sit in the green wood, and to watch the Sun in his chariot of gold, and the Moon in her chariot of pearl. Sweet is the scent of the hawthorn, and sweet are the bluebells that hide in the valley, and the heather that blows on the hill. Yet Love is better than Life, and what is the heart of a bird compared to the heart of a man?"

So she spread her brown wings for flight, and soared into the air. She swept over the garden like a shadow, and like a shadow she sailed through the grove.

The young Student was still lying on the grass, where she had left him, and the tears were not yet dry in his beautiful eyes.

"Be happy," cried the Nightingale, "be happy; you shall have your red rose. I will build it out of music by moonlight, and stain it with my own heart's-blood. All that I ask of you in return is that you will be a true lover, for Love is wiser than Philosophy, though she is wise, and mightier than Power, though he is mighty. Flame-coloured are his wings, and coloured like flame is his body. His lips are sweet as honey, and his breath is like frankincense."

The Student looked up from the grass, and listened, but he could not understand what the Nightingale was saying to him, for he only knew the things that are written down in books.

But the Oak-tree understood, and felt sad, for he was very fond of the little Nightingale who had built her nest in his branches.

"Sing me one last song," he whispered; "I shall feel very lonely when you are gone."

So the Nightingale sang to the Oak-tree, and her voice was like water bubbling from a silver jar.

When she had finished her song the Student got up, and pulled a note-book and a lead-pencil out of his pocket.

"She has form," he said to himself, as he walked away through the grove – "that cannot be denied to her; but has she got feeling? I am afraid not. In fact, she is like most artists; she is all style, without any sincerity. She would not sacrifice herself for others. She thinks merely of music, and everybody knows that the arts are selfish. Still, it must be admitted that she has some beautiful notes in her voice. What a pity it is that they do not mean anything, or do any practical good." And he went into his room, and lay down on his little pallet-bed, and began to think of his love; and, after a time, he fell asleep.

And when the Moon shone in the heavens the Nightingale flew to the Rose-tree, and set her breast against the thorn. All night long she sang with her breast against the thorn, and the cold crystal Moon leaned down and listened. All night long she sang, and the thorn went deeper and deeper into her breast, and her life-blood ebbed away from her.

She sang first of the birth of love in the heart of a boy and a girl. And on the top-most spray of the Rose-tree there blossomed a marvellous rose, petal following petal, as song followed song. Pale was it, at first, as the mist that hangs over the river – pale as the feet of the morning, and silver as the wings of the dawn. As the shadow of a rose in a mirror of silver, as the shadow of a rose in a water-pool, so was the rose that blossomed on the topmost spray of the Tree.

But the Tree cried to the Nightingale to press closer against the thorn. "Press closer, little Nightingale," cried the Tree, "or the Day will come before the rose is finished."

So the Nightingale pressed closer against the thorn, and louder and louder grew her song, for she sang of the birth of passion in the soul of a man and a maid.

And a delicate flush of pink came into the leaves of the rose, like the flush in the face of the bridegroom when he kisses the lips of the bride. But the thorn had not yet reached her heart, so the rose's heart remained white, for only a Nightingale's heart's-blood can crimson the heart of a rose.

And the Tree cried to the Nightingale to press closer against the thorn. "Press closer, little Nightingale," cried the Tree, "or the Day will come before the rose is finished."

So the Nightingale pressed closer against the thorn, and the thorn touched her heart, and a fierce pang of pain shot through her. Bitter, bitter was the pain, and wilder and wilder grew her song, for she sang of the Love that is perfected by Death, of the Love that dies not in the tomb.

And the marvellous rose became crimson, like the rose of the eastern sky. Crimson was the girdle of petals, and crimson as a ruby was the heart.

But the Nightingale's voice grew fainter, and her little wings began to beat, and a film came over her eyes. Fainter and fainter grew her song, and she felt something choking her in her throat.

Then she gave one last burst of music. The white Moon heard it, and she forgot the dawn, and lingered on in the sky. The red rose heard it, and it trembled all over with ecstasy, and opened its petals to the cold morning air. Echo bore it to her purple cavern in the hills, and woke the sleeping shepherds from their dreams. It floated through the reeds of the river, and they carried its message to the sea.

"Look, look!" cried the Tree, "the rose is finished now;" but the Nightingale made no answer, for she was lying dead in the long grass, with the thorn in her heart.

And at noon the Student opened his window and looked out.

"Why, what a wonderful piece of luck!" he cried; "here is a red rose! I have never seen any rose like it in all my life. It is so beautiful that I am sure it has a long Latin name;" and he leaned down and plucked it.

Then he put on his hat, and ran up to the Professor's house with the rose in his hand.

The daughter of the Professor was sitting in the doorway winding blue silk on a reel, and her little dog was lying at her feet.

"You said that you would dance with me if I brought you a red rose," cried the Student. "Here is the reddest rose in all the world. You will wear it tonight next your heart, and as we dance together it will tell you how I love you."

But the girl frowned.

"I am afraid it will not go with my dress," she answered; "and, besides, the Chamberlain's nephew has sent me some real jewels, and everybody knows that jewels cost far more than flowers."

"Well, upon my word, you are very ungrateful," said the Student angrily; and he threw the rose into the street, where it fell into the gutter, and a cart-wheel went over it.

"Ungrateful!" said the girl. "I tell you what, you are very rude; and, after all, who are you? Only a Student. Why, I don't believe you have even got silver buckles to your shoes as the Chamberlain's nephew has;" and she got up from her chair and went into the house.

"What a silly thing Love is," said the Student as he walked away. "It is not half as useful as Logic, for it does not prove anything, and it is always telling one of things that are not going to happen, and making one believe things that are not true. In fact, it is quite unpractical, and, as in this age to be practical is everything, I shall go back to Philosophy and study Metaphysics."

So he returned to his room and pulled out a great dusty book, and began to read.

The Selfish Giant

Every afternoon, as they were coming from school, the children used to go and play in the Giant's garden.

It was a large lovely garden, with soft green grass. Here and there over the grass stood beautiful flowers like stars, and there were twelve peach-trees that in the spring-time broke out into delicate blossoms of pink and pearl, and in the autumn bore rich fruit. The birds sat on the trees and sang so sweetly that the children used to stop their games in order to listen to them. "How happy we are here!" they cried to each other.

One day the Giant came back. He had been to visit his friend the Cornish ogre, and had stayed with him for seven years. After the seven years were over he had said all that he had to say, for his conversation was limited, and he determined to return to his own castle. When he arrived he saw the children playing in the garden.

"What are you doing here?" he cried in a very gruff voice, and the children ran away.

"My own garden is my own garden," said the Giant; "anyone can understand that, and I will allow nobody to play in it but myself." So he built a high wall all round it, and put up a notice-board.

TRESPASSERS
WILL BE
PROSECUTED

He was a very selfish Giant.

The poor children had now nowhere to play. They tried to play on the road, but the road was very dusty and full of hard stones, and they did not like it. They used to wander round the high wall when their lessons were over, and talk about the beautiful garden inside.

"How happy we were there," they said to each other.

Then the Spring came, and all over the country there were little blossoms and little birds. Only in the garden of the Selfish Giant it was still winter. The birds did not care to sing in it as there were no children, and the trees forgot to blossom. Once a beautiful flower put its head out from the grass, but when it saw the notice-board it was so sorry for the children that it slipped back into the ground again, and went off to sleep. The only people who were pleased were the Snow and the Frost. "Spring has forgotten this garden," they cried, "so we will live here all the year round." The Snow covered up the grass with her great white cloak, and the Frost painted all the trees silver. Then they invited the North Wind to stay with them, and he came. He was wrapped in furs, and he roared all day about the garden, and blew the chimney-pots down. "This is a delightful spot," he said, "we must ask the Hail on a visit." So the Hail came. Every day for three hours he rattled on the roof of the castle till he broke most of the slates, and then he ran round and round the garden as fast as he could go. He was dressed in grey, and his breath was like ice.

"I cannot understand why the Spring is so late in coming," said the Selfish Giant, as he sat at the window and looked out at his cold white garden; "I hope there will be a change in the weather."

But the Spring never came, nor the Summer. The Autumn gave golden fruit to every garden, but to the Giant's garden she gave none. "He is too selfish," she said. So it was always Winter there, and the North Wind, and the Hail, and the Frost, and the Snow danced about through the trees.

One morning the Giant was lying awake in bed when he heard some lovely music. It sounded so sweet to his ears that he thought it must be the King's musicians passing by. It was really only a little linnet singing outside his window, but it was so long since he had heard a bird sing in his garden that it seemed to him to be the most beautiful music in the world. Then the Hail stopped dancing over his head, and the North Wind ceased roaring, and a delicious perfume came to him through the open casement. "I believe the Spring has come at last," said the Giant; and he jumped out of bed and looked out.

What did he see?

He saw a most wonderful sight. Through a little hole in the wall the children had crept in, and they were sitting in the branches of the trees. In every tree that he could see there was a little child. And the trees were so glad to have the children back again that they had covered themselves with blossoms, and were waving their arms gently above the children's heads. The birds were flying about and twittering with delight, and the flowers were looking up through the green grass and laughing. It was a lovely scene, only in one corner it was still winter. It was the farthest corner of the garden, and in it was standing a little boy. He was so small that he could not reach up to the branches of the tree, and he was wandering all round it, crying bitterly. The poor tree was still quite covered with frost and snow, and the North Wind was blowing and roaring above it. "Climb up! little boy," said the Tree, and it bent its branches down as low as it could; but the boy was too tiny.

And the Giant's heart melted as he looked out. "How selfish I have been!" he said; "now I know why the Spring would not come here. I will put that poor little boy on the top of the tree, and then I will knock down the wall, and my garden shall be the children's playground for ever and ever." He was really very sorry for what he had done.

So he crept downstairs and opened the front door quite softly, and went out into the garden. But when the children saw him they were so frightened that they all ran away, and the garden became winter again. Only the little boy did not run, for his eyes were so full of tears that he did not see the Giant coming. And the Giant stole up behind him and took him gently in his hand, and put him up into the tree. And the tree broke at once into blossom, and the birds came and sang on it, and the little boy stretched out his two arms and flung them round the Giant's neck, and kissed him. And the other children, when they saw that the Giant was not wicked any longer, came running back, and with them came the Spring. "It is your garden now, little children," said the Giant, and he took a great axe and knocked down the wall. And when the people were going to market at twelve o'clock they found the Giant playing with the children in the most beautiful garden they had ever seen.

All day long they played, and in the evening they came to the Giant to bid him goodbye.

"But where is your little companion?" he said: "the boy I put into the tree." The Giant loved him the best because he had kissed him.

"We don't know," answered the children; "he has gone away."

"You must tell him to be sure and come here tomorrow," said the Giant. But the children said that they did not know where he lived, and had never seen him before; and the Giant felt very sad.

Every afternoon, when school was over, the children came and played with the Giant. But the little boy whom the Giant loved was never seen again. The Giant was very kind to all the children, yet he longed for his first little friend, and often spoke of him. "How I would like to see him!" he used to say.

Years went over, and the Giant grew very old and feeble. He could not play about any more, so he sat in a huge armchair, and watched the children at their games, and admired his garden. "I have many beautiful flowers," he said; "but the children are the most beautiful flowers of all."

One winter morning he looked out of his window as he was dressing. He did not hate the Winter now, for he knew that it was merely the Spring asleep, and that the flowers were resting.

Suddenly he rubbed his eyes in wonder, and looked and looked. It certainly was a marvellous sight. In the farthest corner of the garden was a tree quite covered with lovely white blossoms. Its branches were all golden, and silver fruit hung down from them, and underneath it stood the little boy he had loved.

Downstairs ran the Giant in great joy, and out into the garden. He hastened across the grass, and came near to the child. And when he came quite close his face grew red with anger, and he said, "Who hath dared to wound thee?" For on the palms of the child's hands were the prints of two nails, and the prints of two nails were on the little feet.

"Who hath dared to wound thee?" cried the Giant; "tell me, that I may take my big sword and slay him."

"Nay!" answered the child; "but these are the wounds of Love."

"Who art thou?" said the Giant, and a strange awe fell on him, and he knelt before the little child.

And the child smiled on the Giant, and said to him, "You let me play once in your garden, today you shall come with me to my garden, which is Paradise."

And when the children ran in that afternoon, they found the Giant lying dead under the tree, all covered with white blossoms.

The Devoted Friend

One morning the old Water-rat put his head out of his hole. He had bright beady eyes and stiff grey whiskers and his tail was like a long bit of black india-rubber. The little ducks were swimming about in the pond, looking just like a lot of yellow canaries, and their mother, who was pure white with real red legs, was trying to teach them how to stand on their heads in the water.

"You will never be in the best society unless you can stand on your heads," she kept saying to them; and every now and then she showed them how it was done. But the little ducks paid no attention to her. They were so young that they did not know what an advantage it is to be in society at all.

"What disobedient children!" cried the old Water-rat; "they really deserve to be drowned."

"Nothing of the kind," answered the Duck, "everyone must make a beginning, and parents cannot be too patient."

"Ah! I know nothing about the feelings of parents," said the Water-rat; "I am not a family man. In fact, I have never been married, and I never intend to be. Love is all very well in its way, but friendship is much higher. Indeed, I know of nothing in the world that is either nobler or rarer than a devoted friendship."

"And what, pray, is your idea of the duties of a devoted friend?" asked a Green Linnet, who was sitting in a willow-tree hard by, and had overheard the conversation.

"Yes, that is just what I want to know," said the Duck; and she swam away to the end of the pond, and stood upon her head, in order to give her children a good example.

"What a silly question!" cried the Water-rat. "I should expect my devoted friend to be devoted to me, of course."

"And what would you do in return?" said the little bird, swinging upon a silver spray, and flapping his tiny wings.

"I don't understand you," answered the Water-rat.

"Let me tell you a story on the subject," said the Linnet.

"Is the story about me?" asked the Water-rat. "If so, I will listen to it, for I am extremely fond of fiction."

"It is applicable to you," answered the Linnet; and he flew down, and alighting upon the bank, he told the story of The Devoted Friend.

"Once upon a time," said the Linnet, "there was an honest little fellow named Hans."

"Was he very distinguished?" asked the Water-rat.

"No," answered the Linnet, "I don't think he was distinguished at all, except for his kind heart, and his funny round good-humoured face. He lived in a tiny cottage all by himself, and every day he worked in his garden. In all the country-side there was no garden so lovely as his. Sweet-william grew there, and Gilly-flowers, and Shepherds'-purses, and Fair-maids of France. There were damask Roses, and yellow Roses, lilac Crocuses, and gold, purple Violets and white. Columbine and Ladysmock, Marjoram and Wild Basil, the Cowslip and the Flower-de-luce, the Daffodil and the Clove-Pink bloomed or blossomed in their proper order as the months went by, one flower taking another flower's place, so that there were always beautiful things to look at, and pleasant odours to smell.

"Little Hans had a great many friends, but the most devoted friend of all was big Hugh the Miller. Indeed, so devoted was the rich Miller to little Hans, that he would never go by his garden without leaning over the wall and plucking a large nosegay, or a handful of sweet herbs, or filling his pockets with plums and cherries if it was the fruit season.

"'Real friends should have everything in common,' the Miller used to say, and little Hans nodded and smiled, and felt very proud of having a friend with such noble ideas.

"Sometimes, indeed, the neighbours thought it strange that the rich Miller never gave little Hans anything in return, though he had a hundred sacks of flour stored away in his mill, and six milch cows, and a large flock of woolly sheep; but Hans never troubled his head about these things, and nothing gave him greater pleasure than to listen to all the wonderful things the Miller used to say about the unselfishness of true friendship.

"So little Hans worked away in his garden. During the spring, the summer, and the autumn he was very happy, but when the winter came, and he had no fruit or flowers to bring to the market, he suffered a good deal from cold and hunger, and often had to go to bed without any supper but a few dried pears or some hard nuts. In the winter, also, he was extremely lonely, as the Miller never came to see him then.

"'There is no good in my going to see little Hans as long as the snow lasts,' the Miller used to say to his wife, 'for when people are in trouble they should be left alone, and not be bothered by visitors. That at least is my idea about friendship, and I am sure I am right. So I shall wait till the spring comes, and then I shall pay him a visit, and he will be able to give me a large basket of primroses and that will make him so happy.'

"'You are certainly very thoughtful about others,' answered the Wife, as she sat in her comfortable armchair by the big pinewood fire; 'very thoughtful indeed. It is quite a treat to hear you talk about friendship. I am sure the clergyman himself could not say such beautiful things as you do, though he does live in a three-storied house, and wear a gold ring on his little finger.'

"'But could we not ask little Hans up here?' said the Miller's youngest son. 'If poor Hans is in trouble I will give him half my porridge, and show him my white rabbits.'

"'What a silly boy you are!' cried the Miller; 'I really don't know what is the use of sending you to school. You seem not to learn anything. Why, if little Hans came up here, and saw our warm fire, and our good supper, and our great cask of red wine, he might get envious, and envy is a most terrible thing, and would spoil anybody's nature. I certainly will not allow Hans' nature to be spoiled. I am his best friend, and I will always watch over him, and see that he is not led into any temptations. Besides, if Hans came here, he might ask me to let him have some flour on credit, and that I could not do. Flour is one thing, and friendship is another, and they should not be confused. Why, the words are spelt differently, and mean quite different things. Everybody can see that.'

"'How well you talk!' said the Miller's Wife, pouring herself out a large glass of warm ale; 'really I feel quite drowsy. It is just like being in church.'

"'Lots of people act well,' answered the Miller; 'but very few people talk well, which shows that talking is much the more difficult thing of the two, and much the finer thing also'; and he looked sternly across the table at his little son, who felt so ashamed of himself that he hung his head down, and grew quite scarlet, and began to cry into his tea. However, he was so young that you must excuse him."

"Is that the end of the story?" asked the Water-rat.

"Certainly not," answered the Linnet, "that is the beginning."

"Then you are quite behind the age," said the Water-rat. "Every good story-teller nowadays starts with the end, and then goes on to the beginning, and concludes with the middle. That is the new method. I heard all about it the other day from a critic who was walking round the pond with a young man. He spoke of the matter at great length, and I am sure he must have been right, for he had blue spectacles and a bald head, and whenever the young man made any remark, he always answered 'Pooh!' But pray go on with your story. I like the Miller immensely. I have all kinds of beautiful sentiments myself, so there is a great sympathy between us."

"Well," said the Linnet, hopping now on one leg and now on the other, "as soon as the winter was over, and the primroses began to open their pale yellow stars, the Miller said to his wife that he would go down and see little Hans.

"'Why, what a good heart you have!' cried his Wife; 'you are always thinking of others. And mind you take the big basket with you for the flowers.'

"So the Miller tied the sails of the windmill together with a strong iron chain, and went down the hill with the basket on his arm.

"'Good morning, little Hans,' said the Miller.

"'Good morning,' said Hans, leaning on his spade, and smiling from ear to ear.

"'And how have you been all the winter?' said the Miller.

"'Well, really,' cried Hans, 'it is very good of you to ask, very good indeed. I am afraid I had rather a hard time of it, but now the spring has come, and I am quite happy, and all my flowers are doing well.'

"'We often talked of you during the winter, Hans,'

said the Miller, 'and wondered how you were getting on.'

"'That was kind of you,' said Hans; 'I was half afraid you had forgotten me.'

"'Hans, I am surprised at you,' said the Miller; 'friendship never forgets. That is the wonderful thing about it, but I am afraid you don't understand the poetry of life. How lovely your primroses are looking, by-the-bye!'"

"'They are certainly very lovely,' said Hans, 'and it is a most lucky thing for me that I have so many. I am going to bring them into the market and sell them to the Burgomaster's daughter, and buy back my wheelbarrow with the money.'

"'Buy back your wheelbarrow? You don't mean to say you have sold it? What a very stupid thing to do!'

"'Well, the fact is,' said Hans, 'that I was obliged to. You see the winter was a very bad time for me, and I really had no money at all to buy bread with. So I first sold the silver buttons off my Sunday coat, and then I sold my silver chain, and then I sold my big pipe, and at last I sold my wheelbarrow. But I am going to buy them all back again now.'

"'Hans,' said the Miller, 'I will give you my wheelbarrow. It is not in very good repair; indeed, one side is gone, and there is something wrong with the wheel-spokes; but in spite of that I will give it to you. I know it is very generous of me, and a great many people would think me extremely foolish for parting with it, but I am not like the rest of the world. I think that generosity is the essence of friendship, and, besides, I have got a new wheelbarrow for myself. Yes, you may set your mind at ease, I will give you my wheelbarrow.'

"'Well, really, that is generous of you,' said little Hans, and his funny round face glowed all over with pleasure. 'I can easily put it in repair, as I have a plank of wood in the house.'

"'A plank of wood!' said the Miller; 'why, that is just what I want for the roof of my barn. There is a very large hole in it, and the corn will all get damp if I don't stop it up. How lucky you mentioned it! It is quite remarkable how one good action always breeds another. I have given you my wheelbarrow, and now you are going to give me your plank. Of course, the wheelbarrow is worth far more than the plank, but true friendship never notices things like that. Pray get it at once, and I will set to work at my barn this very day.'

"'Certainly,' cried little Hans, and he ran into the shed and dragged the plank out.

"'It is not a very big plank,' said the Miller, looking at it, 'and I am afraid that after I have mended my barn-roof there won't be any left for you to mend the wheelbarrow with; but, of course, that is not my fault. And now, as I have given you my wheelbarrow, I am sure you would like to give me some flowers in return. Here is the basket, and mind you fill it quite full.'

"'Quite full?' said little Hans, rather sorrowfully, for it was really a very big basket, and he knew that if he filled it he would have no flowers left for the market and he was very anxious to get his silver buttons back.

"'Well, really,' answered the Miller, 'as I have given you my wheelbarrow, I don't think that it is much to ask you for a few flowers. I may be wrong, but I should have thought that friendship, true friendship, was quite free from selfishness of any kind.'

"'My dear friend, my best friend,' cried little Hans, 'you are welcome to all the flowers in my garden. I would much sooner have your good opinion than my silver buttons, any day'; and he ran and plucked all his pretty primroses, and filled the Miller's basket.

"'Goodbye, little Hans,' said the Miller, as he went up the hill with the plank on his shoulder, and the big basket in his hand.

"'Goodbye,' said little Hans, and he began to dig away quite merrily, he was so pleased about the wheelbarrow.

"The next day he was nailing up some honeysuckle against the porch, when he heard the Miller's voice calling to him from the road. So he jumped off the ladder, and ran down the garden, and looked over the wall.

"There was the Miller with a large sack of flour on his back.

"'Dear little Hans,' said the Miller, 'would you mind carrying this sack of flour for me to market?'

"'Oh, I am so sorry,' said Hans, 'but I am really very busy today. I have got all my creepers to nail up, and all my flowers to water, and all my grass to roll.'

"'Well, really,' said the Miller, 'I think that, considering that I am going to give you my wheelbarrow, it is rather unfriendly of you to refuse.'

"'Oh, don't say that,' cried little Hans, 'I wouldn't be unfriendly for the whole world'; and he ran in for his cap, and trudged off with the big sack on his shoulders.

"It was a very hot day, and the road was terribly dusty, and before Hans had reached the sixth milestone he was so tired that he had to sit down and rest. However, he went on bravely, and as last he reached the market. After he had waited there some time, he sold the sack of flour for a very good price, and then he returned home at once, for he was afraid that if he stopped too late he might meet some robbers on the way.

"'It has certainly been a hard day,' said little Hans to himself as he was going to bed, 'but I am glad I did not refuse the Miller, for he is my best friend, and, besides, he is going to give me his wheelbarrow.'

"Early the next morning the Miller came down to get the money for his sack of flour, but little Hans was so tired that he was still in bed.

"'Upon my word,' said the Miller, 'you are very lazy. Really, considering that I am going to give you my wheelbarrow, I think you might work harder. Idleness is a great sin, and I certainly don't like any of my friends to be idle or sluggish. You must not mind my speaking quite plainly to you. Of course I should not dream of doing so if I were not your friend. But what is the good of friendship if one cannot say exactly what one means? Anybody can say charming things and try to please and to flatter, but a true friend always says unpleasant things, and does not mind giving pain. Indeed, if he is a really true friend he prefers it, for he knows that then he is doing good.'

"'I am very sorry,' said little Hans, rubbing his eyes and pulling off his night-cap, 'but I was so tired that I thought I would lie in bed for a little time, and listen to the birds singing. Do you know that I always work better after hearing the birds sing?'

"'Well, I am glad of that,' said the Miller, clapping little Hans on the back, 'for I want you to come up to the mill as soon as you are dressed, and mend my barn-roof for me.'

"Poor little Hans was very anxious to go and work in his garden, for his flowers had not been watered for two days, but he did not like to refuse the Miller, as he was such a good friend to him.

"'Do you think it would be unfriendly of me if I said I was busy?' he inquired in a shy and timid voice.

"'Well, really,' answered the Miller, 'I do not think it is much to ask of you, considering that I am going to give you my wheelbarrow; but of course if you refuse I will go and do it myself.'

"'Oh! on no account,' cried little Hans and he jumped out of bed, and dressed himself, and went up to the barn.

"He worked there all day long, till sunset, and at sunset the Miller came to see how he was getting on.

"'Have you mended the hole in the roof yet, little Hans?' cried the Miller in a cheery voice.

"'It is quite mended,' answered little Hans, coming down the ladder.

"'Ah!' said the Miller, 'there is no work so delightful as the work one does for others.'

"'It is certainly a great privilege to hear you talk,' answered little Hans, sitting down, and wiping his forehead, 'a very great privilege. But I am afraid I shall never have such beautiful ideas as you have.'

"'Oh! they will come to you,' said the Miller, 'but you must take more pains. At present you have only the practice of friendship; some day you will have the theory also.'

"'Do you really think I shall?' asked little Hans.

"'I have no doubt of it,' answered the Miller, 'but now that you have mended the roof, you had better go home and rest, for I want you to drive my sheep to the mountain tomorrow.'

"Poor little Hans was afraid to say anything to this, and early the next morning the Miller brought his sheep round to the cottage, and Hans started off with them to the mountain. It took him the whole day to get there and back; and when he returned he was so tired that he went off to sleep in his chair, and did not wake up till it was broad daylight.

"'What a delightful time I shall have in my garden,' he said, and he went to work at once.

"But somehow he was never able to look after his flowers at all, for his friend the Miller was always coming round and sending him off on long errands, or getting him to help at the mill. Little Hans was very much distressed at times, as he was afraid his flowers would think he had forgotten them, but he consoled himself by the reflection that the Miller was his best friend. 'Besides,' he used to say, 'he is going to give me his wheelbarrow, and that is an act of pure generosity.'

"So little Hans worked away for the Miller, and the Miller said all kinds of beautiful things about friendship, which Hans took down in a note-book, and used to read over at night, for he was a very good scholar.

"Now it happened that one evening little Hans was sitting by his fireside when a loud rap came at the door. It was a very wild night, and the wind was blowing and roaring round the house so terribly that at first he thought it was merely the storm. But a second rap came, and then a third, louder than any of the others.

"'It is some poor traveller,' said little Hans to himself, and he ran to the door.

"There stood the Miller with a lantern in one hand and a big stick in the other.

"'Dear little Hans,' cried the Miller, 'I am in great trouble. My little boy has fallen off a ladder and hurt himself, and I am going for the Doctor. But he lives so far away, and it is such a bad night, that it has just occurred to me that it would be much better if you went instead of me. You know I am going to give you my wheelbarrow, and so, it is only fair that you should do something for me in return.'

"'Certainly,' cried little Hans, 'I take it quite as a compliment your coming to me, and I will start off at once. But you must lend me your lantern, as the night is so dark that I am afraid I might fall into the ditch.'

"'I am very sorry,' answered the Miller, 'but it is

my new lantern, and it would be a great loss to me if anything happened to it.'

"'Well, never mind, I will do without it,' cried little Hans, and he took down his great fur coat, and his warm scarlet cap, and tied a muffler round his throat, and started off.

"What a dreadful storm it was! The night was so black that little Hans could hardly see, and the wind was so strong that he could scarcely stand. However, he was very courageous, and after he had been walking about three hours, he arrived at the Doctor's house, and knocked at the door.

"'Who is there?' cried the Doctor, putting his head out of his bedroom window.

"'Little Hans, Doctor.'

"'What do you want, little Hans?'

"'The Miller's son has fallen from a ladder, and has hurt himself, and the Miller wants you to come at once.'

"'All right!' said the Doctor; and he ordered his horse, and his big boots, and his lantern, and came downstairs, and rode off in the direction of the Miller's house, little Hans trudging behind him.

"But the storm grew worse and worse, and the rain fell in torrents, and little Hans could not see where he was going, or keep up with the horse. At last he lost his way, and wandered off on the moor, which was a very dangerous place, as it was full of deep holes, and there poor little Hans was drowned. His body was found the next day by some goatherds, floating in a great pool of water, and was brought back by them to the cottage.

"Everybody went to little Hans' funeral, as he was so popular, and the Miller was the chief mourner.

"'As I was his best friend,' said the Miller, 'it is only fair that I should have the best place'; so he walked at the head of the procession in a long black cloak, and every now and then he wiped his eyes with a big pocket-handkerchief.

"'Little Hans is certainly a great loss to everyone,' said the Blacksmith, when the funeral was over, and they were all seated comfortably in the inn, drinking spiced wine and eating sweet cakes.

"'A great loss to me at any rate,' answered the Miller; 'why, I had as good as given him my wheelbarrow, and now I really don't know what to do with it. It is very much in my way at home, and it is in such bad repair that I could not get anything for it if I sold it. I will certainly take care not to give away anything again. One always suffers for being generous.'"

"Well?" said the Water-rat, after a long pause.

"Well, that is the end," said the Linnet.

"But what became of the Miller?" asked the Water-rat.

"Oh! I really don't know," replied the Linnet; "and I am sure that I don't care."

"It is quite evident then that you have no sympathy in your nature," said the Water-rat.

"I am afraid you don't quite see the moral of the story," remarked the Linnet.

"The what?" screamed the Water-rat.

"The moral."

"Do you mean to say that the story has a moral?"

"Certainly," said the Linnet.

"Well, really," said the Water-rat, in a very angry manner, "I think you should have told me that before you began. If you had done so, I certainly would not have listened to you; in fact, I should have said 'Pooh,' like the critic. However, I can say it now;" so he shouted out "Pooh" at the top of his voice, gave a whisk with his tail, and went back into his hole.

"And how do you like the Water-rat?" asked the Duck, who came paddling up some minutes afterwards. "He has a great many good points, but for my own part I have a mother's feelings, and I can never look at a confirmed bachelor without the tears coming into my eyes."

"I am rather afraid that I have annoyed him," answered the Linnet. "The fact is, that I told him a story with a moral."

"Ah! that is always a very dangerous thing to do," said the Duck.

And I quite agree with her.

The Remarkable Rocket

The King's son was going to be married, so there were general rejoicings. He had waited a whole year for his bride, and at last she had arrived. She was a Russian Princess, and had driven all the way from Finland in a sledge drawn by six reindeer. The sledge was shaped like a great golden swan, and between the swan's wings lay the little Princess herself. Her long ermine-cloak reached right down to her feet, on her head was a tiny cap of silver tissue, and she was as pale as the Snow Palace in which she had always lived. So pale was she that as she drove through the streets all the people wondered. "She is like a white rose!" they cried, and they threw down flowers on her from the balconies.

At the gate of the Castle the Prince was waiting to receive her. He had dreamy violet eyes, and his hair was like fine gold. When he saw her he sank upon one knee, and kissed her hand.

"Your picture was beautiful," he murmured, "but you are more beautiful than your picture;" and the little Princess blushed.

"She was like a white rose before," said a young Page

to his neighbour, "but she is like a red rose now;" and the whole Court was delighted.

For the next three days everybody went about saying, "White rose, Red rose, Red rose, White rose;" and the King gave orders that the Page's salary was to be doubled. As he received no salary at all this was not of much use to him, but it was considered a great honour, and was duly published in the Court Gazette.

When the three days were over the marriage was celebrated. It was a magnificent ceremony, and the bride and bridegroom walked hand in hand under a canopy of purple velvet embroidered with little pearls. Then there was a State Banquet, which lasted for five hours. The Prince and Princess sat at the top of the Great Hall and drank out of a cup of clear crystal. Only true lovers could drink out of this cup, for if false lips touched it, it grew grey and dull and cloudy.

"It's quite clear that they love each other," said the little Page, "as clear as crystal!" and the King doubled his salary a second time. "What an honour!" cried all the courtiers.

After the banquet there was to be a Ball. The bride and bridegroom were to dance the Rose-dance together, and the King had promised to play the flute. He played very badly, but no one had ever dared to tell him so, because he was the King. Indeed, he knew only two airs, and was never quite certain which one he was playing; but it made no matter, for, whatever he did, everybody cried out, "Charming! charming!"

The last item on the programme was a grand display

of fireworks, to be let off exactly at midnight. The little Princess had never seen a firework in her life, so the King had given orders that the Royal Pyrotechnist should be in attendance on the day of her marriage.

"What are fireworks like?" she had asked the Prince, one morning, as she was walking on the terrace.

"They are like the Aurora Borealis," said the King, who always answered questions that were addressed to other people, "only much more natural. I prefer them to stars myself, as you always know when they are going to appear, and they are as delightful as my own flute-playing. You must certainly see them."

So at the end of the King's garden a great stand had been set up, and as soon as the Royal Pyrotechnist had put everything in its proper place, the fireworks began to talk to each other.

"The world is certainly very beautiful," cried a little Squib. "Just look at those yellow tulips. Why! if they were real crackers they could not be lovelier. I am very glad I have travelled. Travel improves the mind wonderfully, and does away with all one's prejudices."

"The King's garden is not the world, you foolish squib," said a big Roman Candle; "the world is an enormous place, and it would take you three days to see it thoroughly."

"Any place you love is the world to you," exclaimed a pensive Catherine Wheel, who had been attached to an old deal box in early life, and prided herself on her broken heart; "but love is not fashionable any more, the poets have killed it. They wrote so much about it that nobody believed them, and I am not surprised. True love suffers, and is silent. I remember myself once – But it is no matter now. Romance is a thing of the past."

"Nonsense!" said the Roman Candle, "Romance never dies. It is like the moon, and lives for ever. The bride and bridegroom, for instance, love each other very dearly. I heard all about them this morning from a brown-paper cartridge, who happened to be staying in the same drawer as myself, and knew the latest Court news."

But the Catherine Wheel shook her head. "Romance is dead, Romance is dead, Romance is dead," she murmured. She was one of those people who think that, if you say the same thing over and over a great many times, it becomes true in the end.

Suddenly, a sharp, dry cough was heard, and they all looked round.

It came from a tall, supercilious-looking Rocket, who was tied to the end of a long stick. He always coughed before he made any observation, so as to attract attention.

"Ahem! ahem!" he said, and everybody listened except the poor Catherine Wheel, who was still shaking her head, and murmuring, "Romance is dead."

"Order! order!" cried out a Cracker. He was something of a politician, and had always taken a prominent part in the local elections, so he knew the proper Parliamentary expressions to use.

"Quite dead," whispered the Catherine Wheel, and she went off to sleep.

As soon as there was perfect silence, the Rocket

coughed a third time and began. He spoke with a very slow, distinct voice, as if he was dictating his memoirs, and always looked over the shoulder of the person to whom he was talking. In fact, he had a most distinguished manner.

"How fortunate it is for the King's son," he remarked, "that he is to be married on the very day on which I am to be let off. Really, if it had been arranged beforehand, it could not have turned out better for him; but, Princes are always lucky."

"Dear me!" said the little Squib, "I thought it was quite the other way, and that we were to be let off in the Prince's honour."

"It may be so with you," he answered; "indeed, I have no doubt that it is, but with me it is different. I am a very remarkable Rocket, and come of remarkable parents. My mother was the most celebrated Catherine Wheel of her day, and was renowned for her graceful dancing. When she made her great public appearance she spun round nineteen times before she went out, and each time that she did so she threw into the air seven pink stars. She was three feet and a half in diameter, and made of the very best gunpowder. My father was a Rocket like myself, and of French extraction. He flew so high that the people were afraid that he would never come down again. He did, though, for he was of a kindly disposition, and he made a most brilliant descent in a shower of golden rain. The newspapers wrote about his performance in very flattering terms. Indeed, the Court Gazette called him a triumph of Pylotechnic art."

"Pyrotechnic, Pyrotechnic, you mean," said a Bengal Light; "I know it is Pyrotechnic, for I saw it written on my own canister."

"Well, I said Pylotechnic," answered the Rocket, in a severe tone of voice, and the Bengal Light felt so crushed that he began at once to bully the little squibs, in order to show that he was still a person of some importance.

"I was saying," continued the Rocket, "I was saying – What was I saying?"

"You were talking about yourself," replied the Roman Candle.

"Of course; I knew I was discussing some interesting subject when I was so rudely interrupted. I hate rudeness and bad manners of every kind, for I am extremely sensitive. No one in the whole world is so sensitive as I am, I am quite sure of that."

"What is a sensitive person?" said the Cracker to the Roman Candle.

"A person who, because he has corns himself, always treads on other people's toes," answered the Roman Candle in a low whisper; and the Cracker nearly exploded with laughter.

"Pray, what are you laughing at?" inquired the Rocket; "I am not laughing."

"I am laughing because I am happy," replied the Cracker.

"That is a very selfish reason," said the Rocket angrily. "What right have you to be happy? You should be thinking about others. In fact, you should be thinking about me. I am always thinking about myself, and I expect everybody else to do the same. That is what is called sympathy. It is a beautiful virtue, and I possess it in a high degree. Suppose, for instance, anything happened to me tonight, what a misfortune that would be for everyone! The Prince and Princess would never be happy again, their whole married life would be spoiled; and as for the King, I know he would not get over it. Really, when I begin to reflect on the importance of my position, I am almost moved to tears."

"If you want to give pleasure to others," cried the Roman Candle, "you had better keep yourself dry."

"Certainly," exclaimed the Bengal Light, who was now in better spirits; "that is only common sense."

"Common sense, indeed!" said the Rocket indignantly; "you forget that I am very uncommon, and very remarkable. Why, anybody can have common sense, provided that they have no imagination. But I have imagination, for I never think of things as they really are; I always think of them as being quite different. As for keeping myself dry, there is evidently no one here who can at all appreciate an emotional nature. Fortunately for myself, I don't care. The only thing that sustains one through life is the consciousness of the immense inferiority of everybody else, and this is a feeling that I have always cultivated. But none of you have any hearts. Here you are laughing and making merry just as if the Prince and Princess had not just been married."

"Well, really," exclaimed a small Fire-balloon, "why not? It is a most joyful occasion, and when I soar up into the air I intend to tell the stars all about it. You will

53

see them twinkle when I talk to them about the pretty bride."

"Ah! what a trivial view of life!" said the Rocket; "but it is only what I expected. There is nothing in you; you are hollow and empty. Why, perhaps the Prince and Princess may go to live in a country where there is a deep river, and perhaps they may have one only son, a little fair-haired boy with violet eyes like the Prince himself; and perhaps some day he may go out to walk with his nurse; and perhaps the nurse may go to sleep under a great elder-tree; and perhaps the little boy may fall into the deep river and be drowned. What a terrible misfortune! Poor people, to lose their only son! It is really too dreadful! I shall never get over it."

"But they have not lost their only son," said the Roman Candle; "no misfortune has happened to them at all."

"I never said that they had," replied the Rocket; "I said that they might. If they had lost their only son there would be no use in saying anything more about the matter. I hate people who cry over spilt milk. But when I think that they might lose their only son, I certainly am very much affected."

"You certainly are!" cried the Bengal Light. "In fact, you are the most affected person I ever met."

"You are the rudest person I ever met," said the Rocket, "and you cannot understand my friendship for the Prince."

"Why, you don't even know him," growled the Roman Candle.

"I never said I knew him," answered the Rocket. "I

dare say that if I knew him I should not be his friend at all. It is a very dangerous thing to know one's friends."

"You had really better keep yourself dry," said the Fire-balloon. "That is the important thing."

"Very important for you, I have no doubt," answered the Rocket, "but I shall weep if I choose;" and he actually burst into real tears, which flowed down his stick like rain-drops, and nearly drowned two little beetles, who were just thinking of setting up house together, and were looking for a nice dry spot to live in.

"He must have a truly romantic nature," said the Catherine Wheel, "for he weeps when there is nothing at all to weep about;" and she heaved a deep sigh, and thought about the deal box.

But the Roman Candle and the Bengal Light were quite indignant, and kept saying, "Humbug! humbug!" at the top of their voices. They were extremely practical, and whenever they objected to anything they called it humbug.

Then the moon rose like a wonderful silver shield; and the stars began to shine, and a sound of music came from the palace.

The Prince and Princess were leading the dance. They danced so beautifully that the tall white lilies peeped in at the window and watched them, and the great red poppies nodded their heads and beat time.

Then ten o'clock struck, and then eleven, and then twelve, and at the last stroke of midnight everyone came out on the terrace, and the King sent for the Royal Pyrotechnist.

"Let the fireworks begin," said the King; and the Royal Pyrotechnist made a low bow, and marched down to the end of the garden. He had six attendants with him, each of whom carried a lighted torch at the end of a long pole.

It was certainly a magnificent display.

Whizz! Whizz! went the Catherine Wheel, as she spun round and round. Boom! Boom! went the Roman Candle. Then the Squibs danced all over the place, and the Bengal Lights made everything look scarlet. "Goodbye," cried the Fire-balloon, as he soared away, dropping tiny blue sparks. Bang! Bang! answered the Crackers, who were enjoying themselves immensely. Every one was a great success except the Remarkable Rocket. He was so damp with crying that he could not go off at all. The best thing in him was the gunpowder, and that was so wet with tears that it was of no use. All his poor relations, to whom he would never speak, except with a sneer, shot up into the sky like wonderful golden flowers with blossoms of fire. Huzza! Huzza! cried the Court; and the little Princess laughed with pleasure.

"I suppose they are reserving me for some grand occasion," said the Rocket; "no doubt that is what it means," and he looked more supercilious than ever.

The next day the workmen came to put everything tidy. "This is evidently a deputation," said the Rocket; "I will receive them with becoming dignity" so he put his nose in the air, and began to frown severely as if he were thinking about some very important subject. But they took no notice of him at all till they were just going away. Then one of them caught sight of him. "Hallo!" he cried, "what a bad rocket!" and he threw him over the wall into the ditch.

"BAD Rocket? BAD Rocket?" he said, as he whirled through the air; "impossible! GRAND Rocket, that is what the man said. BAD and GRAND sound very much the same, indeed they often are the same;" and he fell into the mud.

"It is not comfortable here," he remarked, "but no doubt it is some fashionable watering-place, and they have sent me away to recruit my health. My nerves are certainly very much shattered, and I require rest."

Then a little Frog, with bright jewelled eyes, and a green mottled coat, swam up to him.

"A new arrival, I see!" said the Frog. "Well, after all there is nothing like mud. Give me rainy weather and a ditch, and I am quite happy. Do you think it will be a wet afternoon? I am sure I hope so, but the sky is quite blue and cloudless. What a pity!"

"Ahem! ahem!" said the Rocket, and he began to cough.

"What a delightful voice you have!" cried the Frog. "Really it is quite like a croak, and croaking is of course the most musical sound in the world. You will hear our glee-club this evening. We sit in the old duck pond close by the farmer's house, and as soon as the moon rises we begin. It is so entrancing that everybody lies awake to listen to us. In fact, it was only yesterday that I heard the farmer's wife say to her mother that she could not get a wink of sleep at night on account of us. It is most gratifying to find oneself so popular."

"Ahem! ahem!" said the Rocket angrily. He was very much annoyed that he could not get a word in.

"A delightful voice, certainly," continued the Frog; "I hope you will come over to the duck-pond. I am off to look for my daughters. I have six beautiful daughters, and I am so afraid the Pike may meet them. He is a perfect monster, and would have no hesitation in breakfasting off them. Well, goodbye: I have enjoyed our conversation very much, I assure you."

"Conversation, indeed!" said the Rocket. "You have talked the whole time yourself. That is not conversation."

"Somebody must listen," answered the Frog, "and I like to do all the talking myself. It saves time, and prevents arguments."

"But I like arguments," said the Rocket.

"I hope not," said the Frog complacently. "Arguments are extremely vulgar, for everybody in good society holds exactly the same opinions. Goodbye a second time; I see my daughters in the distance;" and the little Frog swam away.

"You are a very irritating person," said the Rocket, "and very ill-bred. I hate people who talk about themselves, as you do, when one wants to talk about oneself, as I do. It is what I call selfishness, and selfishness is a most detestable thing, especially to anyone of my temperament, for I am well known for my sympathetic nature. In fact, you should take example by me; you could not possibly have a better model. Now that you have the chance you had better avail yourself of it, for I am going back to Court almost immediately. I am a great favourite at Court; in fact, the Prince and Princess were married yesterday in my honour. Of course you know nothing of these matters, for you are a provincial."

"There is no good talking to him," said a Dragon-fly, who was sitting on the top of a large brown bulrush; "no good at all, for he has gone away."

"Well, that is his loss, not mine," answered the Rocket. "I am not going to stop talking to him merely because he pays no attention. I like hearing myself talk. It is one of my greatest pleasures. I often have long conversations all by myself, and I am so clever that sometimes I don't understand a single word of what I am saying."

"Then you should certainly lecture on Philosophy," said the Dragon-fly; and he spread a pair of lovely gauze wings and soared away into the sky.

"How very silly of him not to stay here!" said the Rocket. "I am sure that he has not often got such a chance of improving his mind. However, I don't care a bit. Genius like mine is sure to be appreciated some day;" and he sank down a little deeper into the mud.

After some time a large White Duck swam up to him. She had yellow legs, and webbed feet, and was considered a great beauty on account of her waddle.

"Quack, quack, quack," she said. "What a curious shape you are! May I ask were you born like that, or is it the result of an accident?"

"It is quite evident that you have always lived in the

country," answered the Rocket, "otherwise you would know who I am. However, I excuse your ignorance. It would be unfair to expect other people to be as remarkable as oneself. You will no doubt be surprised to hear that I can fly up into the sky, and come down in a shower of golden rain."

"I don't think much of that," said the Duck, "as I cannot see what use it is to anyone. Now, if you could plough the fields like the ox, or draw a cart like the horse, or look after the sheep like the collie-dog, that would be something."

"My good creature," cried the Rocket in a very haughty tone of voice, "I see that you belong to the lower orders. A person of my position is never useful. We have certain accomplishments, and that is more than sufficient. I have no sympathy myself with industry of any kind, least of all with such industries as you seem to recommend. Indeed, I have always been of opinion that hard work is simply the refuge of people who have nothing whatever to do."

"Well, well," said the Duck, who was of a very peaceable disposition, and never quarrelled with anyone, "everybody has different tastes. I hope, at any rate, that you are going to take up your residence here."

"Oh! dear no," cried the Rocket. "I am merely a visitor, a distinguished visitor. The fact is that I find this place rather tedious. There is neither society here, nor solitude. In fact, it is essentially suburban. I shall probably go back to Court, for I know that I am destined to make a sensation in the world."

"I had thoughts of entering public life once myself," remarked the Duck; "there are so many things that need reforming. Indeed, I took the chair at a meeting some time ago, and we passed resolutions condemning everything that we did not like. However, they did not seem to have much effect. Now I go in for domesticity, and look after my family."

"I am made for public life," said the Rocket, "and so are all my relations, even the humblest of them. Whenever we appear we excite great attention. I have not actually appeared myself, but when I do so it will be a magnificent sight. As for domesticity, it ages one rapidly, and distracts one's mind from higher things."

"Ah! the higher things of life, how fine they are!" said the Duck; "and that reminds me how hungry I feel": and she swam away down the stream, saying, "Quack, quack, quack."

"Come back! come back!" screamed the Rocket, "I have a great deal to say to you;" but the Duck paid no attention to him. "I am glad that she has gone," he said to himself, "she has a decidedly middle-class mind;" and he sank a little deeper still into the mud, and began to think about the loneliness of genius, when suddenly two little boys in white smocks came running down the bank, with a kettle and some faggots.

"This must be the deputation," said the Rocket, and he tried to look very dignified.

"Hallo!" cried one of the boys, "look at this old stick! I wonder how it came here;" and he picked the rocket out of the ditch.

"OLD Stick!" said the Rocket, "impossible! GOLD Stick, that is what he said. Gold Stick is very complimentary. In fact, he mistakes me for one of the Court dignitaries!"

"Let us put it into the fire!" said the other boy, "it will help to boil the kettle."

So they piled the faggots together, and put the Rocket on top, and lit the fire.

"This is magnificent," cried the Rocket, "they are going to let me off in broad day-light, so that everyone can see me."

"We will go to sleep now," they said, "and when we wake up the kettle will be boiled;" and they lay down on the grass, and shut their eyes.

The Rocket was very damp, so he took a long time to burn. At last, however, the fire caught him.

"Now I am going off!" he cried, and he made himself very stiff and straight. "I know I shall go much higher than the stars, much higher than the moon, much higher than the sun. In fact, I shall go so high that—"

Fizz! Fizz! Fizz! and he went straight up into the air.

"Delightful!" he cried, "I shall go on like this for ever. What a success I am!"

But nobody saw him.

Then he began to feel a curious tingling sensation all over him.

"Now I am going to explode," he cried. "I shall set the whole world on fire, and make such a noise that nobody will talk about anything else for a whole year."

And he certainly did explode. Bang! Bang! Bang! went the gunpowder. There was no doubt about it.

But nobody heard him, not even the two little boys, for they were sound asleep.

Then all that was left of him was the stick, and this fell down on the back of a Goose who was taking a walk by the side of the ditch.

"Good heavens!" cried the Goose. "It is going to rain sticks;" and she rushed into the water.

"I knew I should create a great sensation," gasped the Rocket, and he went out.

The Star-Child

To
Miss Margot Tennant

Once upon a time two poor Woodcutters were making their way home through a great pine-forest. It was winter, and a night of bitter cold. The snow lay thick upon the ground, and upon the branches of the trees: the frost kept snapping the little twigs on either side of them, as they passed: and when they came to the Mountain-Torrent she was hanging motionless in air, for the Ice-King had kissed her.

So cold was it that even the animals and the birds did not know what to make of it.

"Ugh!" snarled the Wolf, as he limped through the brushwood with his tail between his legs, "this is perfectly monstrous weather. Why doesn't the Government look to it?"

"Weet! weet! weet!" twittered the green Linnets, "the old Earth is dead and they have laid her out in her white shroud."

"The Earth is going to be married, and this is her bridal dress," whispered the Turtle-doves to each other. Their little pink feet were quite frost-bitten, but they felt that it was their duty to take a romantic view of the situation.

"Nonsense!" growled the Wolf. "I tell you that it is all the fault of the Government, and if you don't believe me I shall eat you." The Wolf had a thoroughly practical mind, and was never at a loss for a good argument.

"Well, for my own part," said the Woodpecker, who was a born philosopher, "I don't care an atomic theory for explanations. If a thing is so, it is so, and at present it is terribly cold."

Terribly cold it certainly was. The little Squirrels, who lived inside the tall fir-tree, kept rubbing each other's noses to keep themselves warm, and the Rabbits curled themselves up in their holes, and did not venture even to look out of doors. The only people who seemed to enjoy it were the great horned Owls. Their feathers were quite stiff with rime, but they did not mind, and they rolled their large yellow eyes, and called out to each other across the forest, "Tu-whit! Tu-whoo! Tu-whit! Tu-whoo! what delightful weather we are having!"

On and on went the two Woodcutters, blowing lustily upon their fingers, and stamping with their huge iron-shod boots upon the caked snow. Once they sank into a deep drift, and came out as white as millers are, when the stones are grinding; and once they slipped on the hard smooth ice where the marsh-water was frozen, and their faggots fell out of their bundles, and they had to pick them up and bind them together again; and once they thought that they had lost their way, and a great terror seized on them, for they knew that the Snow is cruel to those who sleep in her arms. But they put their trust in the good Saint Martin, who watches over all travellers, and retraced their steps, and went warily, and at last they reached the outskirts of the forest, and saw, far down in the valley beneath them, the lights of the village in which they dwelt.

So overjoyed were they at their deliverance that they laughed aloud, and the Earth seemed to them like a flower of silver, and the Moon like a flower of gold.

Yet, after that they had laughed they became sad, for they remembered their poverty, and one of them said to the other, "Why did we make merry, seeing that life is for the rich, and not for such as we are? Better that we had died of cold in the forest, or that some wild beast had fallen upon us and slain us."

"Truly," answered his companion, "much is given to some, and little is given to others. Injustice has parcelled out the world, nor is there equal division of aught save of sorrow."

But as they were bewailing their misery to each other this strange thing happened. There fell from heaven a very bright and beautiful star. It slipped down the side of the sky, passing by the other stars in its course, and, as they watched it wondering, it seemed to them to sink behind a clump of willow-trees that stood hard by a little sheepfold no more than a stone's-throw away.

"Why! there is a crook of gold for whoever finds it," they cried, and they set to and ran, so eager were they for the gold.

And one of them ran faster than his mate, and

outstripped him, and forced his way through the willows, and came out on the other side, and lo! there was indeed a thing of gold lying on the white snow. So he hastened towards it, and stooping down placed his hands upon it, and it was a cloak of golden tissue, curiously wrought with stars, and wrapped in many folds. And he cried out to his comrade that he had found the treasure that had fallen from the sky, and when his comrade had come up, they sat them down in the snow, and loosened the folds of the cloak that they might divide the pieces of gold. But, alas! no gold was in it, nor silver, nor, indeed, treasure of any kind, but only a little child who was asleep.

And one of them said to the other: "This is a bitter ending to our hope, nor have we any good fortune, for what doth a child profit to a man? Let us leave it here, and go our way, seeing that we are poor men, and have children of our own whose bread we may not give to another."

But his companion answered him: "Nay, but it were an evil thing to leave the child to perish here in the snow, and though I am as poor as thou art, and have many mouths to feed, and but little in the pot, yet will I bring it home with me, and my wife shall have care of it."

So very tenderly he took up the child, and wrapped the cloak around it to shield it from the harsh cold, and made his way down the hill to the village, his comrade marvelling much at his foolishness and softness of heart.

And when they came to the village, his comrade said to him, "Thou hast the child, therefore give me the cloak, for it is meet that we should share."

But he answered him: "Nay, for the cloak is neither mine nor thine, but the child's only," and he bade him Godspeed, and went to his own house and knocked.

And when his wife opened the door and saw that her husband had returned safe to her, she put her arms round his neck and kissed him, and took from his back the bundle of faggots, and brushed the snow off his boots, and bade him come in.

But he said to her, "I have found something in the forest, and I have brought it to thee to have care of it," and he stirred not from the threshold.

"What is it?" she cried. "Show it to me, for the house is bare, and we have need of many things." And he drew the cloak back, and showed her the sleeping child.

"Alack, goodman!" she murmured, "have we not children of our own, that thou must needs bring a changeling to sit by the hearth? And who knows if it will not bring us bad fortune? And how shall we tend it?" And she was wroth against him.

"Nay, but it is a Star-Child," he answered; and he told her the strange manner of the finding of it.

But she would not be appeased, but mocked at him, and spoke angrily, and cried: "Our children lack bread, and shall we feed the child of another? Who is there who careth for us? And who giveth us food?"

"Nay, but God careth for the sparrows even, and feedeth them," he answered.

"Do not the sparrows die of hunger in the winter?" she asked. "And is it not winter now?"

And the man answered nothing, but stirred not from the threshold.

And a bitter wind from the forest came in through the open door, and made her tremble, and she shivered, and said to him: "Wilt thou not close the door? There cometh a bitter wind into the house, and I am cold."

"Into a house where a heart is hard cometh there not always a bitter wind?" he asked. And the woman answered him nothing, but crept closer to the fire.

And after a time she turned round and looked at him, and her eyes were full of tears. And he came in swiftly, and placed the child in her arms, and she kissed it, and laid it in a little bed where the youngest of their own children was lying. And on the morrow the Woodcutter took the curious cloak of gold and placed it in a great chest, and a chain of amber that was round the child's neck his wife took and set it in the chest also.

So the Star-Child was brought up with the children of the Woodcutter, and sat at the same board with them, and was their playmate. And every year he became more beautiful to look at, so that all those who dwelt in the village were filled with wonder, for, while they were swarthy and black-haired, he was white and delicate as sawn ivory, and his curls were like the rings of the daffodil. His lips, also, were like the petals of a red flower, and his eyes were like violets by a river of pure water, and his body like the narcissus of a field where the mower comes not.

Yet did his beauty work him evil. For he grew proud, and cruel, and selfish. The children of the Woodcutter, and the other children of the village, he despised, saying that they were of mean parentage, while he was noble, being sprang from a Star, and he made himself master over them, and called them his servants. No pity had he for the poor, or for those who were blind or maimed or in any way afflicted, but would cast stones at them and drive them forth on to the highway, and bid them beg their bread elsewhere, so that none save the outlaws came twice to that village to ask for alms. Indeed, he was as one enamoured of beauty, and would mock at the weakly and ill-favoured, and make jest of them; and himself he loved, and in summer, when the winds were still, he would lie by the well in the priest's orchard and look down at the marvel of his own face, and laugh for the pleasure he had in his fairness.

Often did the Woodcutter and his wife chide him, and say: "We did not deal with thee as thou dealest with those who are left desolate, and have none to succour them. Wherefore art thou so cruel to all who need pity?"

Often did the old priest send for him, and seek to teach him the love of living things, saying to him: "The fly is thy brother. Do it no harm. The wild birds that roam through the forest have their freedom. Snare them not for thy pleasure. God made the blind-worm and the mole, and each has its place. Who art thou to bring pain into God's world? Even the cattle of the field praise Him."

71

But the Star-Child heeded not their words, but would frown and flout, and go back to his companions, and lead them. And his companions followed him, for he was fair, and fleet of foot, and could dance, and pipe, and make music. And wherever the Star-Child led them they followed, and whatever the Star-Child bade them do, that did they. And when he pierced with a sharp reed the dim eyes of the mole, they laughed, and when he cast stones at the leper they laughed also. And in all things he ruled them, and they became hard of heart even as he was.

Now there passed one day through the village a poor beggar-woman. Her garments were torn and ragged, and her feet were bleeding from the rough road on which she had travelled, and she was in very evil plight. And being weary she sat her down under a chestnut-tree to rest.

But when the Star-Child saw her, he said to his companions, "See! There sitteth a foul beggar-woman under that fair and green-leaved tree. Come, let us drive her hence, for she is ugly and ill-favoured."

So he came near and threw stones at her, and mocked her, and she looked at him with terror in her eyes, nor did she move her gaze from him. And when the Woodcutter, who was cleaving logs in a haggard hard by, saw what the Star-Child was doing, he ran up and rebuked him, and said to him: "Surely thou art hard of heart and knowest not mercy, for what evil has this poor woman done to thee that thou shouldst treat her in this wise?"

And the Star-Child grew red with anger, and stamped his foot upon the ground, and said, "Who art thou to question me what I do? I am no son of thine to do thy bidding."

"Thou speakest truly," answered the Woodcutter, "yet did I show thee pity when I found thee in the forest."

And when the woman heard these words she gave a loud cry, and fell into a swoon. And the Woodcutter carried her to his own house, and his wife had care of her, and when she rose up from the swoon into which she had fallen, they set meat and drink before her, and bade her have comfort.

But she would neither eat nor drink, but said to the Woodcutter, "Didst thou not say that the child was found in the forest? And was it not ten years from this day?"

And the Woodcutter answered, "Yea, it was in the forest that I found him, and it is ten years from this day."

"And what signs didst thou find with him?" she cried. "Bare he not upon his neck a chain of amber? Was not round him a cloak of gold tissue broidered with stars?"

"Truly," answered the Woodcutter, "it was even as thou sayest." And he took the cloak and the amber chain from the chest where they lay, and showed them to her.

And when she saw them she wept for joy, and said, "He is my little son whom I lost in the forest. I pray thee send for him quickly, for in search of him have I wandered over the whole world."

73

So the Woodcutter and his wife went out and called to the Star-Child, and said to him, "Go into the house, and there shalt thou find thy mother, who is waiting for thee."

So he ran in, filled with wonder and great gladness. But when he saw her who was waiting there, he laughed scornfully and said, "Why, where is my mother? For I see none here but this vile beggar-woman."

And the woman answered him, "I am thy mother."

"Thou art mad to say so," cried the Star-Child angrily. "I am no son of thine, for thou art a beggar, and ugly, and in rags. Therefore get thee hence, and let me see thy foul face no more."

"Nay, but thou art indeed my little son, whom I bare in the forest," she cried, and she fell on her knees, and held out her arms to him. "The robbers stole thee from me, and left thee to die," she murmured, "but I recognised thee when I saw thee, and the signs also have I recognised, the cloak of golden tissue and the amber chain. Therefore I pray thee come with me, for over the whole world have I wandered in search of thee. Come with me, my son, for I have need of thy love."

But the Star-Child stirred not from his place, but shut the doors of his heart against her, nor was there any sound heard save the sound of the woman weeping for pain.

And at last he spoke to her, and his voice was hard and bitter. "If in very truth thou art my mother," he said, "it had been better hadst thou stayed away, and not come here to bring me to shame, seeing that I thought I was the child of some Star, and not a beggar's child, as thou tellest me that I am. Therefore get thee hence, and let me see thee no more."

"Alas! my son," she cried, "wilt thou not kiss me before I go? For I have suffered much to find thee."

"Nay," said the Star-Child, "but thou art too foul to look at, and rather would I kiss the adder or the toad than thee."

So the woman rose up, and went away into the forest weeping bitterly, and when the Star-Child saw that she had gone, he was glad, and ran back to his playmates that he might play with them.

But when they beheld him coming, they mocked him and said, "Why, thou art as foul as the toad, and as loathsome as the adder. Get thee hence, for we will not suffer thee to play with us," and they drave him out of the garden.

And the Star-Child frowned and said to himself, "What is this that they say to me? I will go to the well of water and look into it, and it shall tell me of my beauty."

So he went to the well of water and looked into it, and lo! his face was as the face of a toad, and his body was sealed like an adder. And he flung himself down on the grass and wept, and said to himself, "Surely this has come upon me by reason of my sin. For I have denied my mother, and driven her away, and been proud, and cruel to her. Wherefore I will go and seek her through the whole world, nor will I rest till I have found her."

And there came to him the little daughter of the

Woodcutter, and she put her hand upon his shoulder and said, "What doth it matter if thou hast lost thy comeliness? Stay with us, and I will not mock at thee."

And he said to her, "Nay, but I have been cruel to my mother, and as a punishment has this evil been sent to me. Wherefore I must go hence, and wander through the world till I find her, and she give me her forgiveness."

So he ran away into the forest and called out to his mother to come to him, but there was no answer. All day long he called to her, and, when the sun set he lay down to sleep on a bed of leaves, and the birds and the animals fled from him, for they remembered his cruelty, and he was alone save for the toad that watched him, and the slow adder that crawled past.

And in the morning he rose up, and plucked some bitter berries from the trees and ate them, and took his way through the great wood, weeping sorely. And of everything that he met he made inquiry if perchance they had seen his mother.

He said to the Mole, "Thou canst go beneath the earth. Tell me, is my mother there?"

And the Mole answered, "Thou hast blinded mine eyes. How should I know?"

He said to the Linnet, "Thou canst fly over the tops of the tall trees, and canst see the whole world. Tell me, canst thou see my mother?"

And the Linnet answered, "Thou hast clipt my wings for thy pleasure. How should I fly?"

And to the little Squirrel who lived in the fir-tree, and was lonely, he said, "Where is my mother?"

And the Squirrel answered, "Thou hast slain mine. Dost thou seek to slay thine also?"

And the Star-Child wept and bowed his head, and prayed forgiveness of God's things, and went on through the forest, seeking for the beggar-woman. And on the third day he came to the other side of the forest and went down into the plain.

And when he passed through the villages the children mocked him, and threw stones at him, and the carlots would not suffer him even to sleep in the byres lest he might bring mildew on the stored corn, so foul was he to look at, and their hired men drave him away, and there was none who had pity on him. Nor could he hear anywhere of the beggar-woman who was his mother, though for the space of three years he wandered over the world, and often seemed to see her on the road in front of him, and would call to her, and run after her till the sharp flints made his feet to bleed. But overtake her he could not, and those who dwelt by the way did ever deny that they had seen her, or any like to her, and they made sport of his sorrow.

For the space of three years he wandered over the world, and in the world there was neither love nor loving-kindness nor charity for him, but it was even such a world as he had made for himself in the days of his great pride.

And one evening he came to the gate of a strong-walled city that stood by a river, and, weary and footsore though he was, he made to enter in. But the soldiers who stood on guard dropped their halberts across the entrance, and said roughly to him, "What is thy business in the city?"

"I am seeking for my mother," he answered, "and I pray ye to suffer me to pass, for it may be that she is in this city."

But they mocked at him, and one of them wagged a black beard, and set down his shield and cried, "Of a truth, thy mother will not be merry when she sees thee, for thou art more ill-favoured than the toad of the marsh, or the adder that crawls in the fen. Get thee gone. Get thee gone. Thy mother dwells not in this city."

And another, who held a yellow banner in his hand, said to him, "Who is thy mother, and wherefore art thou seeking for her?"

And he answered, "My mother is a beggar even as I am, and I have treated her evilly, and I pray ye to suffer me to pass that she may give me her forgiveness, if it be that she tarrieth in this city." But they would not, and pricked him with their spears.

And, as he turned away weeping, one whose armour was inlaid with gilt flowers, and on whose helmet couched a lion that had wings, came up and made inquiry of the soldiers who it was who had sought entrance. And they said to him, "It is a beggar and the child of a beggar, and we have driven him away."

"Nay," he cried, laughing, "but we will sell the foul thing for a slave, and his price shall be the price of a bowl of sweet wine."

And an old and evil-visaged man who was passing by

called out, and said, "I will buy him for that price," and, when he had paid the price, he took the Star-Child by the hand and led him into the city.

And after that they had gone through many streets they came to a little door that was set in a wall that was covered with a pomegranate tree. And the old man touched the door with a ring of graved jasper and it opened, and they went down five steps of brass into a garden filled with black poppies and green jars of burnt clay. And the old man took then from his turban a scarf of figured silk, and bound with it the eyes of the Star-Child, and drave him in front of him. And when the scarf was taken off his eyes, the Star-Child found himself in a dungeon, that was lit by a lantern of horn.

And the old man set before him some mouldy bread on a trencher and said, "Eat," and some brackish water in a cup and said, "Drink," and when he had eaten and drunk, the old man went out, locking the door behind him and fastening it with an iron chain.

And on the morrow the old man, who was indeed the subtlest of the magicians of Libya and had learned his art from one who dwelt in the tombs of the Nile, came in to him and frowned at him, and said, "In a wood that is nigh to the gate of this city of Giaours there are three pieces of gold. One is of white gold, and another is of yellow gold, and the gold of the third one is red. Today thou shalt bring me the piece of white gold, and if thou bringest it not back, I will beat thee with a hundred stripes. Get thee away quickly, and at sunset I will be waiting for thee at the door of the garden. See that thou bringest the white gold, or it shall go ill with thee, for thou art my slave, and I have bought thee for the price of a bowl of sweet wine." And he bound the eyes of the Star-Child with the scarf of figured silk, and led him through the house, and through the garden of poppies, and up the five steps of brass. And having opened the little door with his ring he set him in the street.

And the Star-Child went out of the gate of the city, and came to the wood of which the Magician had spoken to him.

Now this wood was very fair to look at from without, and seemed full of singing birds and of sweet-scented flowers, and the Star-Child entered it gladly. Yet did its beauty profit him little, for wherever he went harsh briars and thorns shot up from the ground and encompassed him, and evil nettles stung him, and the thistle pierced him with her daggers, so that he was in sore distress. Nor could he anywhere find the piece of white gold of which the Magician had spoken, though he sought for it from morn to noon, and from noon to sunset. And at sunset he set his face towards home, weeping bitterly, for he knew what fate was in store for him.

But when he had reached the outskirts of the wood, he heard from a thicket a cry as of someone in pain. And forgetting his own sorrow he ran back to the place, and saw there a little Hare caught in a trap that some hunter had set for it.

And the Star-Child had pity on it, and released it,

and said to it, "I am myself but a slave, yet may I give thee thy freedom."

And the Hare answered him, and said: "Surely thou hast given me freedom, and what shall I give thee in return?"

And the Star-Child said to it, "I am seeking for a piece of white gold, nor can I anywhere find it, and if I bring it not to my master he will beat me."

"Come thou with me," said the Hare, "and I will lead thee to it, for I know where it is hidden, and for what purpose."

So the Star-Child went with the Hare, and lo! in the cleft of a great oak-tree he saw the piece of white gold that he was seeking. And he was filled with joy, and seized it, and said to the Hare, "The service that I did to thee thou hast rendered back again many times over, and the kindness that I showed thee thou hast repaid a hundred-fold."

"Nay," answered the Hare, "but as thou dealt with me, so I did deal with thee," and it ran away swiftly, and the Star-Child went towards the city.

Now at the gate of the city there was seated one who was a leper. Over his face hung a cowl of grey linen, and through the eyelets his eyes gleamed like red coals. And when he saw the Star-Child coming, he struck upon a wooden bowl, and clattered his bell, and called out to him, and said, "Give me a piece of money, or I must die of hunger. For they have thrust me out of the city, and there is no one who has pity on me."

"Alas!" cried the Star-Child, "I have but one piece of

money in my wallet, and if I bring it not to my master he will beat me, for I am his slave."

But the leper entreated him, and prayed of him, till the Star-Child had pity, and gave him the piece of white gold.

And when he came to the Magician's house, the Magician opened to him, and brought him in, and said to him, "Hast thou the piece of white gold?" And the Star-Child answered, "I have it not." So the Magician fell upon him, and beat him, and set before him an empty trencher, and said, "Eat," and an empty cup, and said, "Drink," and flung him again into the dungeon.

And on the morrow the Magician came to him, and said, "If today thou bringest me not the piece of yellow gold, I will surely keep thee as my slave, and give thee three hundred stripes."

So the Star-Child went to the wood, and all day long he searched for the piece of yellow gold, but nowhere could he find it. And at sunset he sat him down and began to weep, and as he was weeping there came to him the little Hare that he had rescued from the trap.

And the Hare said to him, "Why art thou weeping? And what dost thou seek in the wood?"

And the Star-Child answered, "I am seeking for a piece of yellow gold that is hidden here, and if I find it not my master will beat me, and keep me as a slave."

"Follow me," cried the Hare, and it ran through the wood till it came to a pool of water. And at the bottom of the pool the piece of yellow gold was lying.

"How shall I thank thee?" said the Star-Child, "for lo! this is the second time that you have succoured me."

"Nay, but thou hadst pity on me first," said the Hare, and it ran away swiftly.

And the Star-Child took the piece of yellow gold, and put it in his wallet, and hurried to the city. But the leper saw him coming, and ran to meet him, and knelt down and cried, "Give me a piece of money or I shall die of hunger."

And the Star-Child said to him, "I have in my wallet but one piece of yellow gold, and if I bring it not to my master he will beat me and keep me as his slave."

But the leper entreated him sore, so that the Star-Child had pity on him, and gave him the piece of yellow gold.

And when he came to the Magician's house, the Magician opened to him, and brought him in, and said to him, "Hast thou the piece of yellow gold?" And the Star-Child said to him, "I have it not." So the Magician fell upon him, and beat him, and loaded him with chains, and cast him again into the dungeon.

And on the morrow the Magician came to him, and said, "If today thou bringest me the piece of red gold I will set thee free, but if thou bringest it not I will surely slay thee."

So the Star-Child went to the wood, and all day long he searched for the piece of red gold, but nowhere could he find it. And at evening he sat him down and wept, and as he was weeping there came to him the little Hare.

And the Hare said to him, "The piece of red gold that thou seekest is in the cavern that is behind thee. Therefore weep no more but be glad."

"How shall I reward thee?" cried the Star-Child, "for lo! this is the third time thou hast succoured me."

"Nay, but thou hadst pity on me first," said the Hare, and it ran away swiftly.

And the Star-Child entered the cavern, and in its farthest corner he found the piece of red gold. So he put it in his wallet, and hurried to the city. And the leper seeing him coming, stood in the centre of the road, and cried out, and said to him, "Give me the piece of red money, or I must die," and the Star-Child had pity on him again, and gave him the piece of red gold, saying, "Thy need is greater than mine." Yet was his heart heavy, for he knew what evil fate awaited him.

But lo! as he passed through the gate of the city, the guards bowed down and made obeisance to him, saying, "How beautiful is our lord!" and a crowd of citizens followed him, and cried out, "Surely there is none so beautiful in the whole world!" so that the Star-Child wept, and said to himself, "They are mocking me, and making light of my misery." And so large was the concourse of the people, that he lost the threads of his way, and found himself at last in a great square, in which there was a palace of a King.

And the gate of the palace opened, and the priests and the high officers of the city ran forth to meet him, and they abased themselves before him, and said, "Thou art our lord for whom we have been waiting, and the son of our King."

And the Star-Child answered them and said, "I am no king's son, but the child of a poor beggar-woman. And how say ye that I am beautiful, for I know that I am evil to look at?"

Then he, whose armour was inlaid with gilt flowers, and on whose helmet crouched a lion that had wings, held up a shield, and cried, "How saith my lord that he is not beautiful?"

And the Star-Child looked, and lo! his face was even as it had been, and his comeliness had come back to him, and he saw that in his eyes which he had not seen there before.

And the priests and the high officers knelt down and said to him, "It was prophesied of old that on this day should come he who was to rule over us. Therefore, let our lord take this crown and this sceptre, and be in his justice and mercy our King over us."

But he said to them, "I am not worthy, for I have denied the mother who bare me, nor may I rest till I have found her, and known her forgiveness. Therefore, let me go, for I must wander again over the world, and may not tarry here, though ye bring me the crown and the sceptre." And as he spake he turned his face from them towards the street that led to the gate of the city, and lo! amongst the crowd that pressed round the soldiers, he saw the beggar-woman who was his mother, and at her side stood the leper, who had sat by the road.

And a cry of joy broke from his lips, and he ran over,

and kneeling down he kissed the wounds on his mother's feet, and wet them with his tears. He bowed his head in the dust, and sobbing, as one whose heart might break, he said to her: "Mother, I denied thee in the hour of my pride. Accept me in the hour of my humility. Mother, I gave thee hatred. Do thou give me love. Mother, I rejected thee. Receive thy child now." But the beggar-woman answered him not a word.

And he reached out his hands, and clasped the white feet of the leper, and said to him: "Thrice did I give thee of my mercy. Bid my mother speak to me once." But the leper answered him not a word.

And he sobbed again and said: "Mother, my suffering is greater than I can bear. Give me thy forgiveness, and let me go back to the forest." And the beggar-woman put her hand on his head, and said to him, "Rise," and the leper put his hand on his head, and said to him, "Rise," also.

And he rose up from his feet, and looked at them, and lo! they were a King and a Queen.

And the Queen said to him, "This is thy father whom thou hast succoured."

And the King said, "This is thy mother whose feet thou hast washed with thy tears." And they fell on his neck and kissed him, and brought him into the palace and clothed him in fair raiment, and set the crown upon his head, and the sceptre in his hand, and over the city that stood by the river he ruled, and was its lord. Much justice and mercy did he show to all, and the evil Magician he banished, and to the Woodcutter and his wife he sent many rich gifts, and to their children he gave high honour. Nor would he suffer any to be cruel to bird or beast, but taught love and loving-kindness and charity, and to the poor he gave bread, and to the naked he gave raiment, and there was peace and plenty in the land.

Yet ruled he not long, so great had been his suffering, and so bitter the fire of his testing, for after the space of three years he died. And he who came after him ruled evilly.

The Canterville Ghost

I.

When Mr Hiram B. Otis, the American Minister, bought Canterville Chase, every one told him he was doing a very foolish thing, as there was no doubt at all that the place was haunted. Indeed, Lord Canterville himself, who was a man of the most punctilious honour, had felt it his duty to mention the fact to Mr Otis when they came to discuss terms.

"We have not cared to live in the place ourselves," said Lord Canterville, "since my grand-aunt, the Dowager Duchess of Bolton, was frightened into a fit, from which she never really recovered, by two skeleton hands being placed on her shoulders as she was dressing for dinner, and I feel bound to tell you, Mr Otis, that the ghost has been seen by several living members of my family, as well as by the rector of the parish, the Rev. Augustus Dampier, who is a Fellow of King's College, Cambridge. After the unfortunate accident to the Duchess, none of our younger servants would stay with us, and Lady Canterville often got very little sleep at night, in consequence of the mysterious noises that came from the corridor and the library."

"My Lord," answered the Minister, "I will take the furniture and the ghost at a valuation. I have come from a modern country, where we have everything that money can buy; and with all our spry young fellows painting the Old World red, and carrying off your best actors and prima-donnas, I reckon that if there were such a thing as a ghost in Europe, we'd have it at home in a very short time in one of our public museums, or on the road as a show."

"I fear that the ghost exists," said Lord Canterville, smiling, "though it may have resisted the overtures of your enterprising impresarios. It has been well known for three centuries, since 1584 in fact, and always makes its appearance before the death of any member of our family."

"Well, so does the family doctor for that matter, Lord Canterville. But there is no such thing, sir, as a ghost, and I guess the laws of Nature are not going to be suspended for the British aristocracy."

"You are certainly very natural in America," answered Lord Canterville, who did not quite understand Mr Otis's last observation, "and if you don't mind a ghost in the house, it is all right. Only you must remember I warned you."

A few weeks after this, the purchase was concluded, and at the close of the season the Minister and his family went down to Canterville Chase. Mrs Otis, who, as Miss Lucretia R. Tappan, of West 53rd Street, had been a celebrated New York belle, was now a very handsome, middle-aged woman, with fine eyes, and a superb profile. Many American ladies on leaving their native land adopt an appearance of chronic ill-health, under the impression that it is a form of European refinement, but Mrs Otis had never fallen into this error. She had a magnificent constitution, and a really wonderful amount of animal spirits. Indeed, in many respects, she was quite English, and was an excellent example of the fact that we have really everything in common with America nowadays, except, of course, language. Her eldest son, christened Washington by his parents in a moment of patriotism, which he never ceased to regret, was a fair-haired, rather good-looking young man, who had qualified himself for American diplomacy by leading the German at the Newport Casino for three successive seasons, and even in London was well known as an excellent dancer. Gardenias and the peerage were his only weaknesses. Otherwise he was extremely sensible. Miss Virginia E. Otis was a little girl of fifteen, lithe and lovely as a fawn, and with a fine freedom in her large blue eyes. She was a wonderful Amazon, and had once raced old Lord Bilton on her pony twice round the park, winning by a length and a half, just in front of the Achilles statue, to the huge delight of the young Duke of Cheshire, who proposed for her on the spot, and was sent back to Eton that very night by his guardians, in floods of tears. After Virginia came the twins, who were usually called "The Star and Stripes," as they were always getting swished. They were delightful boys, and, with the exception of the worthy Minister, the only true republicans of the family.

As Canterville Chase is seven miles from Ascot, the nearest railway station, Mr Otis had telegraphed for a waggonette to meet them, and they started on their drive in high spirits. It was a lovely July evening, and the air was delicate with the scent of the pinewoods. Now and then they heard a wood-pigeon brooding over its own sweet voice, or saw, deep in the rustling fern, the burnished breast of the pheasant. Little squirrels peered at them from the beech-trees as they went by, and the rabbits scudded away through the brushwood and over the mossy knolls, with their white tails in the air. As they entered the avenue of Canterville Chase, however, the sky became suddenly overcast with clouds, a curious stillness seemed to hold the atmosphere, a great flight of rooks passed silently over their heads, and, before they reached the house, some big drops of rain had fallen.

Standing on the steps to receive them was an old woman, neatly dressed in black silk, with a white cap and apron. This was Mrs Umney, the housekeeper, whom Mrs Otis, at Lady Canterville's earnest request, had consented to keep in her former position. She made them each a low curtsey as they alighted, and said in a quaint, old-fashioned manner, "I bid you welcome to Canterville Chase." Following her, they passed through the fine Tudor hall into the library, a long, low room, panelled in black oak, at the end of which was a large stained glass window. Here they found tea laid out for them, and, after taking off their wraps, they sat down and began to look round, while Mrs Umney waited on them.

Suddenly Mrs Otis caught sight of a dull red stain on the floor just by the fireplace, and, quite unconscious of what it really signified, said to Mrs Umney, "I am afraid something has been spilt there."

"Yes, madam," replied the old housekeeper in a low voice, "blood has been spilt on that spot."

"How horrid!" cried Mrs Otis; "I don't at all care for blood-stains in a sitting-room. It must be removed at once."

The old woman smiled, and answered in the same low, mysterious voice, "It is the blood of Lady Eleanore de Canterville, who was murdered on that very spot by her own husband, Sir Simon de Canterville, in 1575. Sir Simon survived her nine years, and disappeared suddenly under very mysterious circumstances. His body has never been discovered, but his guilty spirit still haunts the Chase. The blood-stain has been much admired by tourists and others, and cannot be removed."

"That is all nonsense," cried Washington Otis; "Pinkerton's Champion Stain Remover and Paragon Detergent will clean it up in no time," and before the terrified housekeeper could interfere, he had fallen upon his knees, and was rapidly scouring the floor with a small stick of what looked like a black cosmetic. In a few moments no trace of the blood-stain could be seen.

"I knew Pinkerton would do it," he exclaimed, triumphantly, as he looked round at his admiring family; but no sooner had he said these words than a terrible flash of lightning lit up the sombre room, a fearful peal of thunder made them all start to their feet, and Mrs Umney fainted.

"What a monstrous climate!" said the American Minister, calmly, as he lit a long cheroot. "I guess the old country is so overpopulated that they have not enough decent weather for everybody. I have always been of opinion that emigration is the only thing for England."

"My dear Hiram," cried Mrs Otis, "what can we do with a woman who faints?"

"Charge it to her like breakages," answered the Minister; "she won't faint after that;" and in a few moments Mrs Umney certainly came to. There was no doubt, however, that she was extremely upset, and she sternly warned Mr Otis to beware of some trouble coming to the house.

"I have seen things with my own eyes, sir," she said, "that would make any Christian's hair stand on end, and many and many a night I have not closed my eyes in sleep for the awful things that are done here." Mr Otis, however, and his wife warmly assured the honest soul that they were not afraid of ghosts, and, after invoking the blessings of Providence on her new master and mistress, and making arrangements for an increase of salary, the old housekeeper tottered off to her own room.

II.

The storm raged fiercely all that night, but nothing of particular note occurred. The next morning, however, when they came down to breakfast, they found the terrible stain of blood once again on the floor. "I don't think it can be the fault of the Paragon Detergent," said Washington, "for I have tried it with everything. It must be the ghost." He accordingly rubbed out the stain a second time, but the second morning it appeared again. The third morning also it was there, though the library had been locked up at night by Mr Otis himself, and the key carried upstairs. The whole family were now quite interested; Mr Otis began to suspect that he had been too dogmatic in his denial of the existence of ghosts, Mrs Otis expressed her intention of joining the Psychical Society, and Washington prepared a long letter to Messrs. Myers and Podmore on the subject of the Permanence of Sanguineous Stains when connected with Crime. That night all doubts about the objective existence of phantasmata were removed for ever.

The day had been warm and sunny; and, in the cool of the evening, the whole family went out to drive. They did not return home till nine o'clock, when they had a light supper. The conversation in no way turned upon ghosts, so there were not even those primary conditions of receptive expectations which so often precede the presentation of psychical phenomena. The subjects discussed, as I have since learned from Mr Otis, were merely such as form the ordinary conversation of cultured Americans of the better class, such as the immense superiority of Miss Fanny Devonport over Sarah Bernhardt as an actress; the difficulty of obtaining green corn, buckwheat cakes, and hominy, even in the best English houses; the importance of Boston in the development of the world-soul; the advantages of the baggage-check system in railway travelling; and the sweetness of the New York accent as compared to the London drawl. No mention at all was made of the supernatural, nor was Sir Simon de Canterville alluded to in any way. At eleven o'clock the family retired, and by half-past all the lights were out. Some time after, Mr Otis was awakened by a curious noise in the corridor, outside his room. It sounded like the clank of metal, and seemed to be coming nearer every moment. He got up at once, struck a match, and looked at the time. It was exactly one o'clock. He was quite calm, and felt his pulse, which was not at all feverish. The strange noise still continued, and with it he heard distinctly the sound of footsteps. He put on his slippers, took a small oblong phial out of his dressing-case, and opened the door. Right in front of him he saw, in the wan moonlight, an old man of terrible aspect. His eyes were as red burning coals; long grey hair fell over his shoulders in matted coils; his garments, which were of antique cut, were soiled and ragged, and from his wrists and ankles hung heavy manacles and rusty gyves.

"My dear sir," said Mr Otis, "I really must insist on your oiling those chains, and have brought you for that purpose a small bottle of the Tammany Rising Sun Lubricator. It is said to be completely efficacious upon one application, and there are several testimonials to that effect on the wrapper from some of our most eminent native divines. I shall leave it here for you by the bedroom candles, and will be happy to supply you with more, should you require it." With these words the

United States Minister laid the bottle down on a marble table, and, closing his door, retired to rest.

For a moment the Canterville ghost stood quite motionless in natural indignation; then, dashing the bottle violently upon the polished floor, he fled down the corridor, uttering hollow groans, and emitting a ghastly green light. Just, however, as he reached the top of the great oak staircase, a door was flung open, two little white-robed figures appeared, and a large pillow whizzed past his head! There was evidently no time to be lost, so, hastily adopting the Fourth Dimension of Space as a means of escape, he vanished through the wainscoting, and the house became quite quiet.

On reaching a small secret chamber in the left wing, he leaned up against a moonbeam to recover his breath, and began to try and realize his position. Never, in a brilliant and uninterrupted career of three hundred years, had he been so grossly insulted. He thought of the Dowager Duchess, whom he had frightened into a fit as she stood before the glass in her lace and diamonds; of the four housemaids, who had gone into hysterics when he merely grinned at them through the curtains on one of the spare bedrooms; of the rector of the parish, whose candle he had blown out as he was coming late one night from the library, and who had been under the care of Sir William Gull ever since, a perfect martyr to nervous disorders; and of old Madame de Tremouillac, who, having wakened up one morning early and seen a skeleton seated in an armchair by the fire reading her diary, had been confined to her bed for six weeks with an attack of brain fever, and, on her recovery, had become reconciled to the Church, and broken off her connection with that notorious sceptic, Monsieur de Voltaire. He remembered the terrible night when the wicked Lord Canterville was found choking in his dressing-room, with the knave of diamonds half-way down his throat, and confessed, just before he died, that he had cheated Charles James Fox out of £50,000 at Crockford's by means of that very card, and swore that the ghost had made him swallow it. All his great achievements came back to him again, from the butler who had shot himself in the pantry because he had seen a green hand tapping at the window-pane, to the beautiful Lady Stutfield, who was always obliged to wear a black velvet band round her throat to hide the mark of five fingers burnt upon her white skin, and who drowned herself at last in the carp-pond at the end of the King's Walk. With the enthusiastic egotism of the true artist, he went over his most celebrated performances, and smiled bitterly to himself as he recalled to mind his last appearance as "Red Reuben, or the Strangled Babe," his *début* as "Guant Gibeon, the Blood-sucker of Bexley Moor," and the *furore* he had excited one lovely June evening by merely playing ninepins with his own bones upon the lawn-tennis ground. And after all this some wretched modern Americans were to come and offer him the Rising Sun Lubricator, and throw pillows at his head! It was quite unbearable. Besides, no ghost in history had ever been treated in this manner. Accordingly, he determined to have vengeance, and remained till daylight in an attitude of deep thought.

III.

The next morning, when the Otis family met at breakfast, they discussed the ghost at some length. The United States Minister was naturally a little annoyed to find that his present had not been accepted. "I have no wish," he said, "to do the ghost any personal injury, and I must say that, considering the length of time he has been in the house, I don't think it is at all polite to throw pillows at him," – a very just remark, at which, I am sorry to say, the twins burst into shouts of laughter. "Upon the other hand," he continued, "if he really declines to use the Rising Sun Lubricator, we shall have to take his chains from him. It would be quite impossible to sleep, with such a noise going on outside the bedrooms."

For the rest of the week, however, they were undisturbed, the only thing that excited any attention being the continual renewal of the blood-stain on the library floor. This certainly was very strange, as the door was always locked at night by Mr Otis, and the windows kept closely barred. The chameleon-like colour, also, of the stain excited a good deal of comment. Some mornings it was a dull (almost Indian) red, then it would be vermilion, then a rich purple, and once when they came down for family prayers, according to the simple rites of the Free American Reformed Episcopalian

Church, they found it a bright emerald-green. These kaleidoscopic changes naturally amused the party very much, and bets on the subject were freely made every evening. The only person who did not enter into the joke was little Virginia, who, for some unexplained reason, was always a good deal distressed at the sight of the blood-stain, and very nearly cried the morning it was emerald-green.

The second appearance of the ghost was on Sunday night. Shortly after they had gone to bed they were suddenly alarmed by a fearful crash in the hall. Rushing downstairs, they found that a large suit of old armour had become detached from its stand, and had fallen on the stone floor, while seated in a high-backed chair was the Canterville ghost, rubbing his knees with an expression of acute agony on his face. The twins, having brought their pea-shooters with them, at once discharged two pellets on him, with that accuracy of aim which can only be attained by long and careful practice on a writing-master, while the United States Minister covered him with his revolver, and called upon him, in accordance with Californian etiquette, to hold up his hands! The ghost started up with a wild shriek of rage, and swept through them like a mist, extinguishing Washington Otis's candle as he passed, and so leaving them all in total darkness. On reaching the top of the staircase he recovered himself, and determined to give his celebrated peal of demoniac laughter. This he had on more than one occasion found extremely useful. It was said to have turned Lord Raker's wig grey in a single night, and had certainly made three of Lady Canterville's French governesses give warning before their month was up. He accordingly laughed his most horrible laugh, till the old vaulted roof rang and rang again, but hardly had the fearful echo died away when a door opened, and Mrs Otis came out in a light blue dressing-gown. "I am afraid you are far from well," she said, "and have brought you a bottle of Doctor Dobell's tincture. If it is indigestion, you will find it a most excellent remedy." The ghost glared at her in fury, and began at once to make preparations for turning himself into a large black dog, an accomplishment for which he was justly renowned, and to which the family doctor always attributed the permanent idiocy of Lord Canterville's uncle, the Hon. Thomas Horton. The sound of approaching footsteps, however, made him hesitate in his fell purpose, so he contented himself with becoming faintly phosphorescent, and vanished with a deep churchyard groan, just as the twins had come up to him.

On reaching his room he entirely broke down, and became a prey to the most violent agitation. The vulgarity of the twins, and the gross materialism of Mrs Otis, were naturally extremely annoying, but what really distressed him most was that he had been unable to wear the suit of mail. He had hoped that even modern Americans would be thrilled by the sight of a Spectre in armour, if for no more sensible reason, at least out of respect for their natural poet Longfellow, over whose graceful and attractive poetry he himself had whiled away many a weary hour when the Cantervilles were up in town. Besides it was his own suit. He had worn it with great success at the Kenilworth tournament, and had been highly complimented on it by no less a person than the Virgin Queen herself. Yet when he had put it on, he had been completely overpowered by the weight of the huge breastplate and steel casque, and had fallen heavily on the stone pavement, barking both his knees severely, and bruising the knuckles of his right hand.

For some days after this he was extremely ill, and hardly stirred out of his room at all, except to keep the blood-stain in proper repair. However, by taking great care of himself, he recovered, and resolved to make a third attempt to frighten the United States Minister and his family. He selected Friday, August 17th, for his appearance, and spent most of that day in looking over his wardrobe, ultimately deciding in favour of a large slouched hat with a red feather, a winding-sheet frilled at the wrists and neck, and a rusty dagger. Towards evening a violent storm of rain came on, and the wind was so high that all the windows and doors in the old house shook and rattled. In fact, it was just such weather as he loved. His plan of action was this. He was to make his way quietly to Washington Otis's room, gibber at him from the foot of the bed, and stab himself three times in the throat to the sound of low music. He bore Washington a special grudge, being quite aware that it was he who was in the habit of removing the famous Canterville blood-stain by means of Pinkerton's Paragon Detergent. Having reduced the reckless and foolhardy youth to a condition of abject terror, he was then to proceed to the room occupied by the United States Minister and his wife, and there to place a clammy hand on Mrs Otis's forehead, while he hissed into her trembling husband's ear the awful secrets of the charnel-house. With regard to little Virginia, he had not quite made up his mind. She had never insulted him in any way, and was pretty and gentle. A few hollow groans from the wardrobe, he thought, would be more than sufficient, or, if that failed to wake her, he might grabble at the counterpane with palsy-twitching fingers. As for the twins, he was quite determined to teach them a lesson. The first thing to be done was, of course, to sit upon their chests, so as to produce the stifling sensation of nightmare. Then, as their beds were quite close to each other, to stand between them in the form of a green, icy-cold corpse, till they became paralyzed with fear, and finally, to throw off the winding-sheet, and crawl round the room, with white, bleached bones and one rolling eyeball, in the character of "Dumb Daniel, or the Suicide's Skeleton," a *rôle* in which he had on more than one occasion produced a great effect, and which he considered quite equal to his famous part of "Martin the Maniac, or the Masked Mystery."

At half-past ten he heard the family going to bed. For some time he was disturbed by wild shrieks of laughter from the twins, who, with the light-hearted gaiety of schoolboys, were evidently amusing themselves before they retired to rest, but at a quarter-past eleven all was still, and, as midnight sounded, he sallied forth. The owl beat against the window-panes, the raven croaked from the old yew-tree, and the wind wandered moaning round the house like a lost soul; but the Otis family slept unconscious of their doom, and high above the rain and storm he could hear the steady snoring of the Minister for the United States. He stepped stealthily out of the wainscoting, with an evil smile on his cruel, wrinkled mouth, and the moon hid her face in a cloud as he stole past the great oriel window, where his own arms and those of his murdered wife were blazoned in azure and gold. On and on he glided, like an evil shadow, the very darkness seeming to loathe him as he passed. Once he thought he heard something call, and stopped; but it was only the baying of a dog from the Red Farm, and he went on, muttering strange sixteenth-century curses, and ever and anon brandishing the rusty dagger in the midnight air. Finally he reached the corner of the passage that led to luckless Washington's room. For a moment he paused there, the wind blowing his long grey locks about his head, and twisting into grotesque and fantastic folds the nameless horror of the dead man's shroud. Then the clock struck the quarter, and he felt the time was come. He chuckled to himself, and turned the corner; but no sooner had he done so than, with a piteous wail of terror, he fell back, and hid his blanched face in his long, bony hands. Right in front of him was standing a horrible spectre, motionless as a carven image, and monstrous as a madman's dream! Its head was bald and burnished; its face round, and fat, and white; and hideous laughter seemed to have writhed its features into an eternal grin. From the eyes streamed rays of scarlet light, the mouth was a wide well of fire, and a hideous garment, like to his own, swathed with its silent snows the Titan form. On its breast was a placard with strange writing in antique characters, some scroll of shame it seemed, some record of wild sins, some awful calendar of crime, and, with its right hand, it bore aloft a falchion of gleaming steel.

Never having seen a ghost before, he naturally was terribly frightened, and, after a second hasty glance at the awful phantom, he fled back to his room, tripping up in his long winding-sheet as he sped down the corridor, and finally dropping the rusty dagger into the Minister's jack-boots, where it was found in the morning by the butler. Once in the privacy of his own apartment, he flung himself down on a small pallet-bed, and hid his face under the clothes. After a time, however, the brave old Canterville spirit asserted itself, and he determined to go and speak to the other ghost as soon as it was daylight. Accordingly, just as the dawn was touching the hills with silver, he returned towards the spot where he had first laid eyes on the grisly phantom, feeling that, after all, two ghosts were better than one, and that, by the aid of his new friend, he might safely grapple with the twins. On reaching the spot, however, a terrible sight met his gaze. Something had evidently happened to the spectre, for the light had entirely faded from its hollow eyes, the gleaming falchion had fallen from its hand, and it was leaning up against the wall in a strained and uncomfortable attitude. He rushed forward and seized it in his arms, when, to his horror, the head slipped off and rolled on the floor, the body assumed a recumbent posture, and he found himself clasping a white dimity bed-curtain, with a sweeping-brush, a kitchen cleaver, and a hollow turnip lying at his feet! Unable to understand this curious transformation, he clutched the placard with feverish haste, and there, in the grey morning light, he read these fearful words:

YE OTIS GHOSTE

Ye Onlie True and Originale Spook.
Beware of Ye Imitationes.
All others are Counterfeite.

The whole thing flashed across him. He had been tricked, foiled, and out-witted! The old Canterville look came into his eyes; he ground his toothless gums together; and, raising his withered hands high above his head, swore according to the picturesque phraseology of the antique school, that, when Chanticleer had sounded twice his merry horn, deeds of blood would be wrought, and murder walk abroad with silent feet.

Hardly had he finished this awful oath when, from the red-tiled roof of a distant homestead, a cock crew. He laughed a long, low, bitter laugh, and waited. Hour after hour he waited, but the cock, for some strange reason, did not crow again. Finally, at half-past seven, the arrival of the housemaids made him give up his fearful vigil, and he stalked back to his room, thinking of his vain oath and baffled purpose. There he consulted several books of ancient chivalry, of which he was exceedingly fond, and found that, on every occasion on which this oath had been used, Chanticleer had always crowed a second time. "Perdition seize the naughty fowl," he muttered, "I have seen the day when, with my stout spear, I would have run him through the gorge, and made him crow for me an 'twere in death!" He then retired to a comfortable lead coffin, and stayed there till evening.

IV.

The next day the ghost was very weak and tired. The terrible excitement of the last four weeks was beginning to have its effect. His nerves were completely shattered, and he started at the slightest noise. For five days he kept his room, and at last made up his mind to give up the point of the blood-stain on the library floor. If the Otis family did not want it, they clearly did not deserve it. They were evidently people on a low, material plane of existence, and quite incapable of appreciating the symbolic value of sensuous phenomena. The question of phantasmic apparitions, and the development of astral bodies, was of course quite a different matter, and really not under his control. It was his solemn duty to appear in the corridor once a week, and to gibber from the large oriel window on the first and third Wednesdays in every month, and he did not see how he could honourably escape from his obligations. It is quite true that his life had been very evil, but, upon the other hand, he was most conscientious in all things connected with the supernatural. For the next three Saturdays, accordingly, he traversed the corridor as usual between midnight and three o'clock, taking every possible precaution against being either heard or seen. He removed his boots, trod as lightly as possible on the old worm-eaten boards, wore a large black velvet cloak, and was careful to use the Rising Sun Lubricator for oiling his chains. I am bound to acknowledge that it was with a good deal of difficulty that he brought himself to adopt this last mode of protection. However, one night, while the family were at dinner, he slipped into Mr Otis's bedroom and carried off the bottle. He felt a little humiliated at first, but afterwards was sensible enough to see that there was a great deal to be said for the invention, and, to a certain degree, it served his purpose. Still in spite of everything he was not left unmolested. Strings were continually being stretched across the corridor, over which he tripped in the dark, and on one occasion, while dressed for the part of "Black Isaac, or the Huntsman of Hogley Woods," he met with a severe fall, through treading on a butter-slide, which the twins had constructed from the entrance of the Tapestry Chamber to the top of the oak staircase. This last insult so enraged him, that he resolved to make one final effort to assert his dignity and social position, and determined to visit the insolent young Etonians the next night in his celebrated character of "Reckless Rupert, or the Headless Earl."

He had not appeared in this disguise for more than seventy years; in fact, not since he had so frightened pretty Lady Barbara Modish by means of it, that she suddenly broke off her engagement with the present Lord Canterville's grandfather, and ran away to Gretna Green with handsome Jack Castletown, declaring that nothing in the world would induce her to marry into a family that allowed such a horrible phantom to walk up and down the terrace at twilight. Poor Jack was afterwards shot in a duel by Lord Canterville on Wandsworth Common, and Lady Barbara died of a broken heart at Tunbridge Wells before the year was out, so, in every way, it had been a great success. It was, however an extremely difficult "make-up," if I may use such a theatrical expression in connection with one of the greatest mysteries of the supernatural, or, to employ a more scientific term, the higher-natural world, and it took him fully three hours to make his preparations. At last everything was ready, and he was very pleased with his appearance. The big leather riding-boots that went with the dress were just a little too large for him, and he could only find one of the two horse-pistols, but, on the whole, he was quite satisfied, and at a quarter-past one he glided out of the wainscoting and crept down the corridor. On reaching the room occupied by the twins, which I should mention was called the Blue Bed Chamber, on account of the colour of its hangings, he found the door just ajar. Wishing to make an effective entrance, he flung it wide open, when a heavy jug of water fell right down on him, wetting him to the skin, and just missing his left shoulder by a couple of inches. At the same moment he heard stifled shrieks of laughter proceeding from the four-post bed. The shock to his nervous system was so great that he fled back to his room as hard as he could go, and the next day he was laid up with a severe cold. The only thing that at all consoled him in the whole affair was the fact that he had not brought his head with him, for, had he done so, the consequences might have been very serious.

He now gave up all hope of ever frightening this rude American family, and contented himself, as a rule, with creeping about the passages in list slippers, with a thick red muffler round his throat for fear of draughts, and a small arquebuse, in case he should be attacked by the twins. The final blow he received occurred on the 19th of September. He had gone downstairs to the great entrance-hall, feeling sure that there, at any rate, he would be quite unmolested, and was amusing himself by making satirical remarks on the large Saroni photographs of the United States Minister and his wife which had now taken the place of the Canterville family pictures. He was simply but neatly clad in a long shroud, spotted with churchyard mould, had tied up his jaw with a strip of yellow linen, and carried a small lantern and a sexton's spade. In fact, he was dressed for the character of "Jonas the Graveless, or the Corpse-Snatcher of Chertsey Barn," one of his most remarkable impersonations, and one which the Cantervilles had every reason to remember, as it was the real origin of their quarrel with their neighbour, Lord Rufford. It was about a quarter-past two o'clock in the morning, and, as far as he could ascertain, no one was stirring. As he was strolling towards the library, however, to see if there were any traces left of the blood-stain, suddenly there leaped out on him from a dark corner two figures, who waved their arms wildly above their heads, and shrieked out "BOO!" in his ear.

Seized with a panic, which, under the circumstances, was only natural, he rushed for the staircase, but found Washington Otis waiting for him there with the big garden-syringe, and being thus hemmed in by his enemies on every side, and driven almost to bay, he vanished into the great iron stove, which, fortunately for him, was not lit, and had to make his way home through the flues and chimneys, arriving at his own room in a terrible state of dirt, disorder, and despair.

After this he was not seen again on any nocturnal expedition. The twins lay in wait for him on several occasions, and strewed the passages with nutshells every night to the great annoyance of their parents and the servants, but it was of no avail. It was quite evident that his feelings were so wounded that he would not appear. Mr Otis consequently resumed his great work on the history of the Democratic Party, on which he had been engaged for some years; Mrs Otis organized a wonderful clam-bake, which amazed the whole county; the boys took to lacrosse euchre, poker, and other American national games, and Virginia rode about the lanes on her pony, accompanied by the young Duke of Cheshire, who had come to spend the last week of his holidays at Canterville Chase. It was generally assumed that the ghost had gone away, and, in fact, Mr Otis wrote a letter to that effect to Lord Canterville, who, in reply, expressed his great pleasure at the news, and sent his best congratulations to the Minister's worthy wife.

The Otises, however, were deceived, for the ghost was still in the house, and though now almost an invalid, was by no means ready to let matters rest, particularly as he heard that among the guests was the young Duke of Cheshire, whose grand-uncle, Lord Francis Stilton, had once bet a hundred guineas with Colonel Carbury that he would play dice with the Canterville ghost, and was found the next morning lying on the floor of the card-room in such a helpless paralytic state that, though he lived on to a great age, he was never able to say anything again but "Double Sixes." The story was well known at the time, though, of course, out of respect to the feelings of the two noble families, every attempt was made to hush it up, and a full account of all the circumstances connected with it will be found in the third volume of Lord Tattle's *Recollections of the Prince Regent and his Friends*. The ghost, then, was naturally very anxious to show that he had not lost his influence over the Stiltons, with whom, indeed, he was distantly connected, his own first cousin having been married *en secondes noces* to the Sieur de Bulkeley, from whom, as every one knows, the Dukes of Cheshire are lineally descended. Accordingly, he made arrangements for appearing to Virginia's little lover in his celebrated impersonation of "The Vampire Monk, or the Bloodless Benedictine," a performance so horrible that when old Lady Startup saw it, which she did on one fatal New Year's Eve, in the year 1764, she went off into the most piercing shrieks, which culminated in violent apoplexy, and died in three days, after disinheriting the Cantervilles, who were her nearest relations, and leaving all her money to her London apothecary. At the last moment, however, his terror of the twins prevented his leaving his room, and the little Duke slept in peace under the great feathered canopy in the Royal Bedchamber, and dreamed of Virginia.

V.

A few days after this, Virginia and her curly-haired cavalier went out riding on Brockley meadows, where she tore her habit so badly in getting through a hedge that, on their return home, she made up her mind to go up by the back staircase so as not to be seen. As she was running past the Tapestry Chamber, the door of which happened to be open, she fancied she saw some one inside, and thinking it was her mother's maid, who sometimes used to bring her work there, looked in to ask her to mend her habit. To her immense surprise, however, it was the Canterville Ghost himself! He was sitting by the window, watching the ruined gold of the yellowing trees fly through the air, and the red leaves dancing madly down the long avenue. His head was leaning on his hand, and his whole attitude was one of extreme depression. Indeed, so forlorn, and so much out of repair did he look, that little Virginia, whose first idea had been to run away and lock herself in her room, was filled with pity, and determined to try and comfort him. So light was her footfall, and so deep his melancholy, that he was not aware of her presence till she spoke to him.

"I am so sorry for you," she said, "but my brothers are going back to Eton tomorrow, and then, if you behave yourself, no one will annoy you."

"It is absurd asking me to behave myself," he answered, looking round in astonishment at the pretty little girl who had ventured to address him, "quite absurd. I must rattle my chains, and groan through keyholes, and walk about at night, if that is what you mean. It is my only reason for existing."

"It is no reason at all for existing, and you know you have been very wicked. Mrs Umney told us, the first day we arrived here, that you had killed your wife."

"Well, I quite admit it," said the Ghost, petulantly, "but it was a purely family matter, and concerned no one else."

"It is very wrong to kill any one," said Virginia, who at times had a sweet puritan gravity, caught from some old New England ancestor.

"Oh, I hate the cheap severity of abstract ethics! My wife was very plain, never had my ruffs properly starched, and knew nothing about cookery. Why, there was a buck I had shot in Hogley Woods, a magnificent pricket, and do you know how she had it sent to table?

However, it is no matter now, for it is all over, and I don't think it was very nice of her brothers to starve me to death, though I did kill her."

"Starve you to death? Oh, Mr Ghost – I mean Sir Simon, are you hungry? I have a sandwich in my case. Would you like it?"

"No, thank you, I never eat anything now; but it is very kind of you, all the same, and you are much nicer than the rest of your horrid, rude, vulgar, dishonest family."

"Stop!" cried Virginia, stamping her foot, "it is you who are rude, and horrid, and vulgar, and as for dishonesty, you know you stole the paints out of my box to try and furbish up that ridiculous blood-stain in the library. First you took all my reds, including the vermilion, and I couldn't do any more sunsets, then you took the emerald-green and the chrome-yellow, and finally I had nothing left but indigo and Chinese white, and could only do moonlight scenes, which are always depressing to look at, and not at all easy to paint. I never told on you, though I was very much annoyed, and it was most ridiculous, the whole thing; for who ever heard of emerald-green blood?"

"Well, really," said the Ghost, rather meekly, "what was I to do? It is a very difficult thing to get real blood nowadays, and, as your brother began it all with his Paragon Detergent, I certainly saw no reason why I should not have your paints. As for colour, that is always a matter of taste: the Cantervilles have blue blood, for instance, the very bluest in England; but I know you Americans don't care for things of this kind."

"You know nothing about it, and the best thing you can do is to emigrate and improve your mind. My father will be only too happy to give you a free passage, and though there is a heavy duty on spirits of every kind, there will be no difficulty about the Custom House, as the officers are all Democrats. Once in New York, you are sure to be a great success. I know lots of people there who would give a hundred thousand dollars to have a grandfather, and much more than that to have a family ghost."

"I don't think I should like America."

"I suppose because we have no ruins and no curiosities," said Virginia, satirically.

"No ruins! no curiosities!" answered the Ghost; "you have your navy and your manners."

"Good evening; I will go and ask papa to get the twins an extra week's holiday."

"Please don't go, Miss Virginia," he cried; "I am so lonely and so unhappy, and I really don't know what to do. I want to go to sleep and I cannot."

"That's quite absurd! You have merely to go to bed and blow out the candle. It is very difficult sometimes to keep awake, especially at church, but there is no difficulty at all about sleeping. Why, even babies know how to do that, and they are not very clever."

"I have not slept for three hundred years," he said sadly, and Virginia's beautiful blue eyes opened in wonder; "for three hundred years I have not slept, and I am so tired."

Virginia grew quite grave, and her little lips trembled like rose-leaves. She came towards him, and kneeling

116

down at his side, looked up into his old withered face.

"Poor, poor Ghost," she murmured; "have you no place where you can sleep?"

"Far away beyond the pine-woods," he answered, in a low, dreamy voice, "there is a little garden. There the grass grows long and deep, there are the great white stars of the hemlock flower, there the nightingale sings all night long. All night long he sings, and the cold crystal moon looks down, and the yew-tree spreads out its giant arms over the sleepers."

Virginia's eyes grew dim with tears, and she hid her face in her hands.

"You mean the Garden of Death," she whispered.

"Yes, Death. Death must be so beautiful. To lie in the soft brown earth, with the grasses waving above one's head, and listen to silence. To have no yesterday, and no tomorrow. To forget time, to forget life, to be at peace. You can help me. You can open for me the portals of Death's house, for Love is always with you, and Love is stronger than Death is."

Virginia trembled, a cold shudder ran through her, and for a few moments there was silence. She felt as if she was in a terrible dream.

Then the ghost spoke again, and his voice sounded like the sighing of the wind.

"Have you ever read the old prophecy on the library window?"

"Oh, often," cried the little girl, looking up; "I know it quite well. It is painted in curious black letters, and is difficult to read. There are only six lines:

WHEN A GOLDEN GIRL CAN WIN
PRAYER FROM OUT THE LIPS OF SIN,
WHEN THE BARREN ALMOND BEARS,
AND A LITTLE CHILD GIVES AWAY ITS TEARS,
THEN SHALL ALL THE HOUSE BE STILL
AND PEACE COME TO CANTERVILLE.

But I don't know what they mean."

"They mean," he said, sadly, "that you must weep with me for my sins, because I have no tears, and pray with me for my soul, because I have no faith, and then, if you have always been sweet, and good, and gentle, the angel of death will have mercy on me. You will see fearful shapes in darkness, and wicked voices will whisper in your ear, but they will not harm you, for against the purity of a little child the powers of Hell cannot prevail."

Virginia made no answer, and the ghost wrung his hands in wild despair as he looked down at her bowed golden head. Suddenly she stood up, very pale, and with a strange light in her eyes. "I am not afraid," she said firmly, "and I will ask the Angel to have mercy on you."

He rose from his seat with a faint cry of joy, and taking her hand bent over it with old-fashioned grace and kissed it. His fingers were as cold as ice, and his lips burned like fire, but Virginia did not falter, as he led her across the dusky room. On the faded green tapestry were broidered little huntsmen. They blew their tasselled horns and with their tiny hands waved to her to go back. "Go back! little Virginia," they cried, "go back!" but the ghost clutched her hand more tightly, and she shut her eyes against them. Horrible animals with lizard tails and goggle eyes blinked at her from the carven chimneypiece, and murmured, "Beware! little Virginia, beware! we may never see you again," but the Ghost glided on more swiftly, and Virginia did not listen. When they reached the end of the room he stopped, and muttered some words she could not understand. She opened her eyes, and saw the wall slowly fading away like a mist, and a great black cavern in front of her. A bitter cold wind swept round them, and she felt something pulling at her dress. "Quick, quick," cried the Ghost, "or it will be too late," and in a moment the wainscoting had closed behind them, and the Tapestry Chamber was empty.

VI.

About ten minutes later, the bell rang for tea, and, as Virginia did not come down, Mrs Otis sent up one of the footmen to tell her. After a little time he returned and said that he could not find Miss Virginia anywhere. As she was in the habit of going out to the garden every evening to get flowers for the dinner-table, Mrs Otis was not at all alarmed at first, but when six o'clock struck, and Virginia did not appear, she became really agitated, and sent the boys out to look for her, while she herself and Mr Otis searched every room in the house. At half-past six the boys came back and said that they could find no trace of their sister anywhere.

They were all now in the greatest state of excitement, and did not know what to do, when Mr Otis suddenly remembered that, some few days before, he had given a band of gipsies permission to camp in the park. He accordingly at once set off for Blackfell Hollow, where he knew they were, accompanied by his eldest son and two of the farm-servants. The little Duke of Cheshire, who was perfectly frantic with anxiety, begged hard to be allowed to go too, but Mr Otis would not allow him, as he was afraid there might be a scuffle. On arriving at the spot, however, he found that the gipsies had gone, and it was evident that their departure had been rather sudden, as the fire was still burning, and some plates were lying on the grass. Having sent off Washington and the two men to scour the district, he ran home, and despatched telegrams to all the police inspectors in the county, telling them to look out for a little girl who had been kidnapped by tramps or gipsies. He then ordered his horse to be brought round, and, after insisting on his wife and the three boys sitting down to dinner, rode off down the Ascot road with a groom. He had hardly, however, gone a couple of miles, when he heard somebody galloping after him, and, looking round, saw the little Duke coming up on his pony, with his face very flushed, and no hat. "I'm awfully sorry, Mr Otis," gasped out the boy, "but I can't eat any dinner as long as Virginia is lost. Please don't be angry with me; if you had let us be engaged last year, there would never have been all this trouble. You won't send me back, will you? I can't go! I won't go!"

The Minister could not help smiling at the handsome young scapegrace, and was a good deal touched at his devotion to Virginia, so leaning down from his horse, he patted him kindly on the shoulders, and said, "Well, Cecil, if you won't go back, I suppose you must come with me, but I must get you a hat at Ascot."

"Oh, bother my hat! I want Virginia!" cried the little Duke, laughing, and they galloped on to the railway station. There Mr Otis inquired of the station-master if any one answering to the description of Virginia had been seen on the platform, but could get no news of her. The station-master, however, wired up and down the line, and assured him that a strict watch would be kept for her, and, after having bought a hat for the little Duke from a linen-draper, who was just putting up his shutters, Mr Otis rode off to Bexley, a village about four miles away, which he was told was a well-known haunt of the gipsies, as there was a large common next to it. Here they roused up the rural policeman, but could get no information from him, and, after riding all over the common, they turned their horses' heads homewards, and reached the Chase about eleven o'clock, dead-tired and almost heart-broken. They found Washington and the twins waiting for them at the gate-house with lanterns, as the avenue was very dark. Not the slightest trace of Virginia had been discovered. The gipsies had been caught on Brockley meadows, but she was not with them, and they had explained their sudden departure by saying that they had mistaken the date of Chorton Fair, and had gone off in a hurry for fear they should be late. Indeed, they had been quite distressed at hearing of Virginia's disappearance, as they were very grateful to Mr Otis for having allowed them to camp in his park, and four of their number had stayed behind to help in the search. The carp-pond had been dragged, and the whole Chase thoroughly gone over, but without any result. It was evident that, for that night at any rate, Virginia was lost to them; and it was in a state of the deepest depression that Mr Otis and the boys walked up to the house, the groom following behind with the two horses and the pony. In the hall they found a group of frightened servants, and lying on a sofa in the library was poor Mrs Otis, almost out of her mind with terror and anxiety, and having her forehead bathed with eau de cologne by the old housekeeper. Mr Otis at once insisted on her having something to eat, and ordered up supper for the whole party. It was a melancholy meal, as hardly any one spoke, and even the twins were awestruck and subdued, as they were very fond of their sister. When they had finished, Mr Otis, in spite of the entreaties of the little Duke, ordered them all to bed, saying that nothing more could be done that night, and that he would telegraph in the morning to Scotland Yard for some detectives to be sent down immediately. Just as they were passing out of the dining-room, midnight began to boom from the clock tower, and when the last stroke sounded they heard a crash and a sudden shrill cry; a dreadful peal of thunder shook the house, a strain of unearthly music floated through the air, a panel at the top of the staircase flew back with a loud noise, and out on the landing, looking very pale and white, with a little casket in her hand, stepped Virginia. In a moment they had all rushed up to her. Mrs Otis clasped her passionately in her arms, the Duke smothered her with violent kisses, and the twins executed a wild war-dance round the group.

"Good heavens! child, where have you been?" said Mr Otis, rather angrily, thinking that she had been playing some foolish trick on them. "Cecil and I have been riding all over the country looking for you, and your mother has been frightened to death. You must never play these practical jokes any more."

"Except on the Ghost! except on the Ghost!" shrieked the twins, as they capered about.

"My own darling, thank God you are found; you must never leave my side again," murmured Mrs Otis, as she kissed the trembling child, and smoothed the tangled gold of her hair.

"Papa," said Virginia, quietly, "I have been with the Ghost. He is dead, and you must come and see him. He had been very wicked, but he was really sorry for all that he had done, and he gave me this box of beautiful jewels before he died."

The whole family gazed at her in mute amazement, but she was quite grave and serious; and, turning round, she led them through the opening in the wainscoting down a narrow secret corridor, Washington following with a lighted candle, which he had caught up from the table. Finally, they came to a great oak door, studded with rusty nails. When Virginia touched it, it swung back on its heavy hinges, and they found themselves in a little low room, with a vaulted ceiling, and one tiny grated window. Imbedded in the wall was a huge iron ring, and chained to it was a gaunt skeleton, that was stretched out at full length on the stone floor, and seemed to be trying to grasp with its long fleshless fingers an old-fashioned trencher and ewer, that were placed just out of its reach. The jug had evidently been once filled with water, as it was covered inside with green mould. There was nothing on the trencher but a pile of dust. Virginia knelt down beside the skeleton, and, folding her little hands together, began to pray silently, while the rest of the party looked on in wonder at the terrible tragedy whose secret was now disclosed to them.

"Hallo!" suddenly exclaimed one of the twins, who had been looking out of the window to try and discover in what wing of the house the room was situated. "Hallo! the old withered almond-tree has blossomed. I can see the flowers quite plainly in the moonlight."

"God has forgiven him," said Virginia, gravely, as she rose to her feet, and a beautiful light seemed to illumine her face.

"What an angel you are!" cried the young Duke, and he put his arm round her neck, and kissed her.

VII.

Four days after these curious incidents, a funeral started from Canterville Chase at about eleven o'clock at night. The hearse was drawn by eight black horses, each of which carried on its head a great tuft of nodding ostrich-plumes, and the leaden coffin was covered by a rich purple pall, on which was embroidered in gold the Canterville coat-of-arms. By the side of the hearse and the coaches walked the servants with lighted torches, and the whole procession was wonderfully impressive. Lord Canterville was the chief mourner, having come up specially from Wales to attend the funeral, and sat in the first carriage along with little Virginia. Then came the United States Minister and his wife, then Washington and the three boys, and in the last carriage was Mrs Umney. It was generally felt that, as she had been frightened by the ghost for more than fifty years of her life, she had a right to see the last of him. A deep grave had been dug in the corner of the churchyard, just under the old yew-tree, and the service was read in the most impressive manner by the Rev. Augustus Dampier. When the ceremony was over, the servants, according to an old custom observed in the Canterville family, extinguished their torches, and, as the coffin was being lowered into the grave, Virginia stepped forward, and laid on it a large cross made of white and pink almond-blossoms. As she did so, the moon came out from behind a cloud, and flooded with its silent silver the little churchyard, and from a distant copse a nightingale began to sing. She thought of the ghost's description of the Garden of Death, her eyes became dim with tears, and she hardly spoke a word during the drive home.

The next morning, before Lord Canterville went up to town, Mr Otis had an interview with him on the subject of the jewels the ghost had given to Virginia. They were perfectly magnificent, especially a certain ruby necklace with old Venetian setting, which was really a superb specimen of sixteenth-century work, and their value was so great that Mr Otis felt considerable scruples about allowing his daughter to accept them.

"My lord," he said, "I know that in this country mortmain is held to apply to trinkets as well as to land, and it is quite clear to me that these jewels are, or should be, heirlooms in your family. I must beg you, accordingly, to take them to London with you, and to regard them simply as a portion of your property which has been restored to you under certain strange conditions. As for my daughter, she is merely a child, and has as yet, I am glad to say, but little interest in such appurtenances of idle luxury. I am also informed by Mrs Otis, who, I may say, is no mean authority upon Art, – having had the privilege of spending several winters in Boston when she was a girl – that these gems are of great monetary worth, and if offered for sale would fetch a tall price. Under these circumstances, Lord Canterville, I feel sure that you will recognize how impossible it would be for me to allow them to remain in the possession of any member of my family; and, indeed, all such vain gauds and toys, however suitable or necessary to the dignity of the British aristocracy, would be completely out of place among those who have been brought up on the severe, and I believe immortal, principles of Republican simplicity. Perhaps I should mention that Virginia is very anxious that you should allow her to retain the box, as a memento of your unfortunate but misguided ancestor. As it is extremely old, and consequently a good deal out of repair, you may perhaps think fit to comply with her request. For my own part, I confess I am a good deal surprised to find a child of mine expressing sympathy with mediævalism in any form, and can only account for it by the fact that Virginia was born in one of your London suburbs shortly after Mrs Otis had returned from a trip to Athens."

Lord Canterville listened very gravely to the worthy Minister's speech, pulling his grey moustache now and then to hide an involuntary smile, and when Mr Otis had ended, he shook him cordially by the hand, and said: "My dear sir, your charming little daughter rendered my unlucky ancestor, Sir Simon, a very important service, and I and my family are much indebted to her for her marvellous courage and pluck. The jewels are clearly hers, and, egad, I believe that if I were heartless enough to take them from her, the wicked old fellow would be out of his grave in a fortnight, leading me the devil of a life. As for their being heirlooms, nothing is an heirloom that is not so mentioned in a will or legal document, and the existence of these jewels has been quite unknown. I assure you I have no more claim on them than your butler, and when Miss Virginia grows up, I dare say she will be pleased to have pretty things to wear. Besides, you forget, Mr Otis, that you took the furniture and the ghost at a valuation, and anything that belonged to the ghost passed at once into your possession, as, whatever activity Sir Simon may have shown in the corridor at night, in point of law he was really dead, and you acquired his property by purchase."

Mr Otis was a good deal distressed at Lord Canterville's refusal, and begged him to reconsider his decision, but the good-natured peer was quite firm, and finally induced the Minister to allow his daughter to retain the present the ghost had given her, and when, in the spring of 1890, the young Duchess of Cheshire was presented at the Queen's first drawing-room on the occasion of her marriage, her jewels were the universal theme of admiration. For Virginia received the coronet, which is the reward of all good little American girls, and was married to her boy-lover as soon as he came of age. They were both so charming, and they loved each other so much, that every one was delighted at the match, except the old Marchioness of Dumbleton, who had tried to catch the Duke for one of her seven unmarried daughters, and had given no less than three expensive dinner-parties for that purpose, and, strange to say, Mr Otis himself. Mr Otis was extremely fond of the young Duke personally, but, theoretically, he objected to titles, and, to use his own words, "was not without apprehension lest, amid the enervating influences of a pleasure-loving aristocracy, the true principles of Republican simplicity should be forgotten." His objections, however, were completely overruled, and I

128

believe that when he walked up the aisle of St George's, Hanover Square, with his daughter leaning on his arm, there was not a prouder man in the whole length and breadth of England.

The Duke and Duchess, after the honeymoon was over, went down to Canterville Chase, and on the day after their arrival they walked over in the afternoon to the lonely churchyard by the pine-woods. There had been a great deal of difficulty at first about the inscription on Sir Simon's tombstone, but finally it had been decided to engrave on it simply the initials of the old gentleman's name, and the verse from the library window. The Duchess had brought with her some lovely roses, which she strewed upon the grave, and after they had stood by it for some time they strolled into the ruined chancel of the old abbey. There the Duchess sat down on a fallen pillar, while her husband lay at her feet smoking a cigarette and looking up at her beautiful eyes. Suddenly he threw his cigarette away, took hold of her hand, and said to her, "Virginia, a wife should have no secrets from her husband."

"Dear Cecil! I have no secrets from you."

"Yes, you have," he answered, smiling, "you have never told me what happened to you when you were locked up with the ghost."

"I have never told any one, Cecil," said Virginia, gravely.

"I know that, but you might tell me."

"Please don't ask me, Cecil, I cannot tell you. Poor Sir Simon! I owe him a great deal. Yes, don't laugh, Cecil, I really do. He made me see what Life is, and what Death signifies, and why Love is stronger than both."

The Duke rose and kissed his wife lovingly.

"You can have your secret as long as I have your heart," he murmured.

"You have always had that, Cecil."

"And you will tell our children some day, won't you?"

Virginia blushed.

The Happy Prince and Other Stories Reading Questions

What makes the first six stories in this collection "fairy tales"? How are they similar or different to other fairy tales you've read?

What was your favourite story in the collection and why?

Why was the prince called the "Happy" prince? Is the Remarkable Rocket really "remarkable"?

"The Canterville Ghost" is not a fairy tale, but rather a longer ghost story of Oscar Wilde's. In what ways does it send up the traditional ghost story?

SCHOLASTIC CLASSICS